Valley of Dragons Book 2: The Lost God

Fanny Garstang

Prologue

Kittal was sat on the sitting room floor in his house in the valley. On the low table was a folded book. Hanging over his shoulders like a monkey was Ozanus, his son, while sat either side of him were two young girls though one was distracted with a kitten under the table. He began to unfold the concertinaed book with its thick cover, "this is the Lord of the Skies, the Great Dragon Lord and this is his sister the Moon Dragon. You can see her when the moon is at its fullest." He glanced to his shoulder where Ozanus' golden brown haired head peered over while his little arms were wrapped round his neck.

Opened before them were some beautiful watercolours of the Gods. The serpentine Dragon Lord was painted with gold leaf curling towards the moon. The moon was painted in a full circle and curved within it was a silver scaled dragon that seemed to shimmer.

"More father, show me the War ones." His son demanded. Kittal smiled, "patience son. Next come the weather Gods, his sons. Without them the days would be dry and hot and nothing would grow. The wind drives the clouds. The Rain God brings the rain and the twin Storm Gods keep the temperature in check." He opened the book further to reveal the Rain God the same dark blue as the eye of a peacock feather. The twins, lightning and thunder, one iridescent purple with a horn on its nose with sparks streaking from it, and the other a dark purple like the clothing dye from crushed beetles, formed a circle around the Rain God. Below them, stretched out with a whisp of cloud caught on his feathered tail was the Wind God painted

3

white with pearl powder to make it shimmer. "And a storm occurs when they squabble with each other."

"Do they fight often?" The elder of the two girls asked.

"They are brothers so they often fight. And here is War and Death, as Ozanus requested."
Unfolding the next two pages a copper plated and black painted God hovered over a landscape that was a battle scene. Both were scarred and blood was painted on their scaled bodies.

"But where there is death there is also life." And he opened the next fold to reveal a blue and green dragon courting, "these two, who are nameless are what ensures the flowers grow, crops become food and animals fatten."

"Make us?" The eldest girl asked with wide eyes, "make the baby in mama's tummy?"

"Yes, without them, we would have none of you." He smiled and drew them closer. One day they would get further into the book to the more obscure and forgotten Gods but for now these were the ones they needed to be aware of. Without them they wouldn't exist as the family they were.

One

The storm had raged for two days. The rain had been relentless and had flooded the courtyards and seeped into the rooms of the palace. It had soaked the tiles and now ran down the walls and dripped from the roof. Fire sparked up and then fizzled out as lightning struck buildings within the city. The court screamed out in fear as the top of the tall pagoda exploded as lightning streaked from the pitch black heavens.

The court huddled in the Empress' audience chamber. Plain dressed servants and gaudy clothed nobles filled the floor and no one could move. Along the walls spear holding guards adjusted their grip nervously as static sparked from their spearheads.

As for the Empress, she sat on her dais straight backed and regally dressed in a high collared bishop sleeved linen underdress with a sleeveless overdress of heavier purple velvet embroidered with flowers and leaves in gold around the edge of the wide skirt and at the waist. Seed pearls were sewn into the embroidery. She looked as if she hadn't been there for two days like the rest of them. Powder and rouge covered old pox scars and wrinkles and ochre dye hid her greying hair.

A smile played on her lips. She loved it when the Gods showed off their immense power, reminding the world below that those on the ground were weak mortals. It had been with their blessing, or so she claimed, that she had taken control of Sunulanda from her weak husband and son.

There was an almighty crash of thunder and the room was suddenly lit with bright white light. Silence and darkness then fell. The rain abruptly stopped. Everyone slowly released their held breaths. They weren't sure whether the world had suddenly ended or whether the storm had run its course.

The court began to stir, to stretch tense limbs, to stand and separate back into their divisions. They all glanced to their Empress for permission to disperse so no one was expecting the roof to suddenly cave in, terracotta tiles and wooden beams raining down and trapping the court. Slowly standing the Empress stared at the mess, ignoring the moans from the injured. Lying in the centre was a naked young man who was shrinking from the size of a giant before her eyes. His skin turned from dark purple, like a body covering bruise, to pink as he stirred. He had crow black hair on his head which trailed down his spine like a horse's mane. A sudden gust of wind blew through the hole, pressing him down. He admitted a howl of pain as invisible claws scrapped down his back.

Two

<u>6 months later</u>

He shook his close shaved head as he harshly said to the novice priestess, "don't talk of freedom or even about being free."

"Why ever not?" She frowned at the slight young man who the Empress kept like a pet in the palace ever since he had fallen through the roof. No one could explain where he had come from or how he had survived the fall, but the Empress was convinced he had fallen from the heavens.

"Because I will never be free. I don't know who I am and I'll carry that knowledge with me to my death sending my spirit into a continuous cycle of rebirth till I discover my memories. But any chance of that will be eroded with every rebirth."

"If you pray to the Gods your questions will be answered." Zhina, dressed in a high-necked grey dress with a square necked pinafore apron over it, cinching the dress in around her waist, remarked with uncompromising devotion. A string of beads engraved with symbols representing each of the Gods hung from the apron straps. Her own shaved head was hidden under a grey head-covering painted with a dragon on it rather than embroidered. A simple white headband on her forehead held the folds of the simple headdress in place.

He tugged at his clothes which even now, 6 months later, he still found strange and uncomfortable. It had taken a week for the servants to convince him to keep his clothes on. Now the tugging had become a nervous tic as he felt restrained by the weight of the light grey shirt and trousers. Over the top he wore a dark grey sleeveless brocade knee length coat with padded shoulders and high collar which hid the scar on his back.

She put a hand on his and he stopped tugging. She always had a calming affect when she was near him… normally. Today something had bothered him, and he was now agitated. Faith in the Dragon Gods made her say, "anything could happen, just give it a chance."

He sank to the floor of the chapel and mournfully remarked, "I know I can't stay trapped here but I don't think I could survive outside these palace walls. I don't think I would know how to." She bit her bottom lip for she understood that feeling sometimes. Being kept hidden away left her with the sense that the walls were closing in on her. But compared to Myrskyr, the name given to him by the Empress, she could escape to the city when that feeling came upon her. He looked up at her, hope shining in his glistening dark blue eyes, "sneak me out with you next time."

"Why would you want to leave this place?" She changed tact, "out there it's horrible and full of poverty and hard work while in here you are treated like a god."

"Only when she is around." He whispered. He glanced nervously around as if his words would get heard by the wrong person.

Zhina knew that the servants treated him poorly when he was not with the Empress. They spat at him and in his food, they slapped and kicked him, and he meekly took it which made them even more determined to get a rise from him. She felt sure the Empress knew but did nothing about it. He tried to hide the tears, but she still saw them. He whispered in a voice so quiet she barely heard him, "she makes me do things at night."

Zhina dared not ask but she knew the Empress' personal priest was often called to the Empress' suite of gaudy decorated rooms. He always looked distressed the day after.

She crouched down and put a hand on his arm. He looked into her face and she saw a scared little boy in his expression. In some ways he was a child as in the first month in the palace he had had to be taught a lot, like a toddler would have to be taught: how to walk, how to eat, how to stay still, how to dress

Cautiously she pulled him to her breast and he released a long shaky sob of angst, "I don't want to live. This isn't my world. I feel like an imposter." He couldn't put a finger on it. All he knew was this palace wasn't where he belonged but the harder he tried to remember the further out of reach it went, "perhaps I should die and then I'll find my way to wherever home is."

He looked up suddenly and saw the descending sun shining on Zhina's face through the chapel's window and he realised he had hidden himself away too long. The Empress would be angry if he didn't appear soon. He pushed away from Zhina and hastily brushed the tears from his face as he stiffly said, "we should return to our places."
She didn't point out she was where she was meant to be, tending the flames of the chapel as only a lowly daughter from a court family could.

It was better than being married and sometimes she enjoyed the awe filled stares she got from others her age. She had freedoms others didn't and the possibility of advancement. It had its shortfalls though, the ugly clothes and loneliness; and perhaps that was why she and Myrskyr had been drawn to each other. Two lonely young people in a court that was centred around pacifying and appeasing their temperamental Empress.

He staggered a little as he got to his feet and then carefully left the room. She watched with concern for under all those clothes he was so thin she felt sure she could feel his bones. He was choosing a long and tortured path to death. She wished there was something she could do for him. Perhaps she should take him to the city streets so he could see the joy in the world?

That night, after the evening blessing had been done, she lay restlessly on her bedroll in her tiny bedroom, dressed in a linen shift and a turban to keep her shaven head warm. Her room was a side chamber to the chapel. She wanted to help Myrskyr somehow and the first thing that came to mind was to get him strong. She crept out of her bed sized room, wrapped a shawl about her slim frame, and walked through the chapel where the painted dragons looked like they had come to life in the light of the sacred flame.

Instinctively she checked the amount of oil in the dish before leaving the room. She made her way down the whitewash servant passages hidden behind the wood panelled corridors for the courtiers towards the kitchens. They also were now quiet, the fires tamped down till morning. She went to the storerooms in search of a raw heart, his favourite.

She winced at the iron smell of blood in the cool room where carcasses hung from large hooks on the ceiling. On a table were lead lined wooden buckets covered in drips of dried blood. Removing the lid from one she found intestines soaking. She tried another and found it full of organs sitting in their blood.

Zhina found a bowl and reached into the bucket for a heart. With it in a bowl she headed back through the palace. She feared she would have to enter the Empress' rooms and be potentially caught by either the woman's servants or guards.

She paused at the door as she heard an angry voice, "what do I need to do to get you to show your true form?"

"Please, I don't understand."

"Mystic, keep going." The Empress demanded.

"No, no. I don't remember." Myrskyr pleaded.

"Awaken oh Lord and bless this deserving woman." The Mystic called out and then Zhina heard someone being hit as bells were rung.

After another half an hour of a naked Myrskyr being thrashed with a leaf covered branch in the centre of a circle of candles while the Mystic's assistant rang bells the Empress called a halt to the process. She knew he was a god, why else would he have fallen through the ceiling of her audience chamber?! She wanted him to reveal who he was but the fall had robbed everything from him. She'd had priests and Mystics from across the country trying to draw the god out but all had failed. In anger she snapped at all three of them, "get out! Get out!"

"Madam…?" The Mystic carefully said.

"What?!" The bells of her filigree headdress jingled in her agitation.

With her distracted Myrskyr scurried from the room and out to

10

the Empress' private garden to hide in the darkness and security
of the vegetation.

Zhina hesitated, did she go after Myrskyr or hear what
the Mystic had to say. She crept closer to the now open door.

"Madam, I think I am the last in the country to be here. If you
really think he is a God then you'll need to go further afield."

"Where?" The Empress eyed the young Mystic suspiciously.

"I have heard of a land across the Sea of Cenfornr..." The
Mystic hesitantly said as if he wasn't careful, he would join other
priests that had disappointed her and would be killed. He glanced
at his Empress from his knees. He could see he had captured her
interest.

She moved a little closer to the edge of her chair, "go on."

"It's a long way..." Was he about to regret this? "It's a country
known as Keytel where the Gods have a man know as the Nejus
as their High Priest."

"As you seem to know this place you are going to go and bring
him back even if you have to bring him back in chains." She
decreed as a smile formed on her face, cracking the dried powder
on it.

"I am honoured." He bowed reluctantly. He should have seen
that coming.

"Now get out of here." The Empress said sternly as she rose to
her feet and two ladies materialised from the shadows to help her
get ready for bed.

Zhina stepped into the shadows as the yellow robed
Mystic and his meek assistant left. He muttered to his assistant,
"damn it. Only the Gods know where he came from and I bet he
isn't one of our Heavenly Lords. Why did I have to be found?"
The assistant said nothing.

She waited till their footsteps had finished echoing on
the tiled floor before entering the private garden via a small door
and passage that bypassed the Empress' chambers. She stood on
the path trying to work out where Myrskyr had hidden.

She heard a sob as the clouds drifted away from the full
moon. By the white light of the moon she spotted Myrskyr
huddled under a bush with his knees up and arms wrapped round

11

them. She slowly approached so as not to startle him.

He glanced up with fear as he heard the footsteps thinking it might be the Empress come to drag him back into her rooms. Like a startled rabbit he made himself ready to flee and looked wary even when he recognised Zhina. She held out the bowl, "I come in peace."

"Go away." He felt humiliation. How much had she seen or heard?

"I did come with a treat for you."

"I said too much today and don't want to talk anymore." He stood, not aware of his nakedness as he couldn't see Zhina blushing. His nose twitched as he smelt the iron reach blood.

"I'm worried for you." She said with concern.

"You're the only one so you shouldn't." He saw her take a step forward and added in an aggressive tone, "don't come any closer."

He wanted to make her afraid of him. He appreciated her friendship but feared what would happen if they became too close. He knew, and hoped she also knew, how easily the Empress became jealous.

He stood taller, un-hunching his shoulders, and stepped into the light of the moon. His hands were fists and he had a stern expression on his face.

She stared at him with horror. He was changing before her eyes. His head went back with a moan and then he dropped to his hands and knees, and his back arched upwards. She cried out, "Myrskyr!"
The face that turned to her wasn't human. His nose had lengthened into a reptilian snout with long drooping whiskers. His almost black hair had grown back and become a feathery mane down his arching back. His eyes widened and his skin had turned dark purple and scaly. The hand that reached for hers had become a four toed claw. A tail curled round. The scars on his back glowed white.

Clouds began to cover the moon again, as if mocking the scene below by removing the moon's healing light before Myrskyr fully formed as a dragon. Myrskyr collapsed on the

12

ground once again as a man. Zhina cried out and then covered her mouth fearing someone would have heard her. She ran from the garden before she was found where she shouldn't be.

Myrskyr came round as the dew settled over the bushes and flowers. He felt exhausted and ached all over but not from being beaten by a branch. His scars itched and felt tight as he stretched his aching back. He knew something had happened to him but couldn't work out what. He felt different and felt he had remembered something about himself but it was evading him again. He felt too tired to stand and crawled back to his bedroll in the Empress' rooms and collapsed on to it.

He didn't stir until the Empress threw a gilded hand mirror at him as she sharply said, "cover yourself."
He rolled on to his side revealing his bony back with a line of hair running down his spine and that his scar had changed. She ignored the fact one of her ladies was doing her hair as she crossed the room with her hair half up. She kicked Myrskyr as she demanded, "what are you hiding from me?"
He turned and grabbed her slippered foot as he hissed, "don't."
She looked at him in horror. He had never touched her or spoken with any aggression. There was a flash of purple scales but she wasn't sure whether she had actually seen it. It had come and gone in the blink of an eye.

She took note of his body then. She had been so determined to bring out the deity she hadn't noticed he had grown thinner and thinner. She could see his ribs and shoulder blades through his pale skin. She saw his muscles tense under his skin as he gripped her foot hard. Her eyes ran over his body to the grim expression on his hollow cheeked face. Her eyes silently challenged him back as she dared him with a sneer of her lips.

She won by default as his hold on her foot dropped away as he fainted. There was definitely something going on. A battle within had only just started though she didn't know what had set it in motion. Now he needed the strength for the battle to continue. She turned to her steward who had just entered with papers for her to look over, "lock him in a room and fetch that

13

Keeper of the Flame that is always hanging around him. She can take care of his every need and get his strength back. If he dies then both of you will too."
The steward's mouth fell open and quickly closed again. He bowed as he hugged the papers, "yes Your Majesty. And the flame?"

"Oh there are plenty of virgins, find another one. Leave those papers you hold and come back in an hour." She held out a hand and accepted the papers before returning to sit before her dressing table, snapping, "hurry up."
Her lady hastened back into her hairdressing role.

　　　The steward stumbled through the corridors and stumbled into the chapel, surprising the Priest and Zhina who were going through morning rituals. The Priest was dressed in a purple and grey brocade robe edged in silver with wide sleeves over baggy unbleached woollen calf length breeches and shirt. On his bald head was a stiff square hat. Like Zhina he wore sandals on his feet. The Priest frowned at the intrusion, "we are not to be disturbed."
Between gasps of air the steward and pointing at Zhina said, "Her Majesty wants her to take care of Myrskyr."
Zhina and the Priest looked at each other. The Priest's glare made Zhina shrink, "what have you been doing? Are you still a virgin?"

"Yes sir. Nothing sir." She protested as she held the bowl of ground incense tight to her chest as a shield.

"Hmm. We'd best obey. Get your things."

"I have nothing." She meekly pointed out.

"Give me your clothes. You are no longer Keeper of the Flame and you'll be given new clothes. You are to tend to Myrskyr's every need." The steward ordered.
With trepidation and excitement she pulled her headdress off and then her dress, grateful she wore a shift underneath against the cold morning air. Cautiously she asked, "what has happened?"

"Only the Gods know. Follow me." The steward answered gruffly.

　　　She was led down the corridors, murmurs following

behind them as servants thought she had disgraced herself. She was shown to a plain plastered room with a bed and bedroll, a table and two chairs, and a long side table which had an empty jug and bowl on it. The steward said, "wait here."

Myrskyr was brought in on a stretcher followed by the court doctor dressed in a black gown. The two men carrying the stretcher lifted Myrskyr on to the bed and then silently left. The doctor eyed Zhina with a lascivious look making her feel ashamed. She knew his arthritic touch tended to wander when he looked after the court ladies. He sneered, "you have fallen far. You really are nothing more than a servant now, just like him." She straightened her back, trying to show him she hadn't been cowered by his look, and asked stiffly, "what do I need to do?"

"Make him eat. See to his every need. Her Majesty wants him fit and well. Give him this mixed with water." The doctor ordered as he placed a clay jar of coarsely ground herbs on the side table, "one spoonful to a cup of water."
He left then and she heard the door lock behind him. She and Myrskyr now seemed to be prisoners.

Three

Keytel

He lay on his front as the doctor from Gloabtona, Lulizen's country of birth, massaged the taut muscles of his scarred shoulders and back. Though Delia had sacrificed herself for him and healed his back there was often a stiffness to his back now. He could hear voices in the house though they sounded muted as he fell asleep under the man's skilled fingers and from the breeze blowing through the open windows of his bedroom.

He was woken by the sounder of laughter. He rolled on to his side with a smile, "what are you two up to? You know you shouldn't be in here."

Two round faced heads, one dark brown haired and the other golden brown, appeared with smiles and a chorus of excitement, "papa!"

"I'm sorry sir, they escaped me again." Their nurse, a young woman from Linyee in a dress and a dress length apron appeared at the door of the bedroom. "come on girls."

They pouted but got to their feet and walked round. Kittal sat up and flexed his shoulders as he swung his trousered legs off the bed. As he saw both of his daughters he sternly said, "come here."

They turned and looked at their father. His tone of voice had been the one they must obey. They approached their father and stared at the floor, hands behind their backs.

With them standing like so he found it hard to remain stern but he had to, "Lylya, Shuang, you should not be running away from your nurse. She is there to take care of you. You should obey her like you do me and your mother."

"Yes papa, sorry papa." They bowed their heads.

"Now go." He said with a small smile, "but only after you've given me a hug."

They looked up with smiles on their faces and ran forward. They climbed on the bed, disturbing a cat that had claimed a free sunny spot on it. They wrapped themselves around their father's bare chest with giggles, oblivious to the scars on his back and left cheek. He put an arm around each one as dark brown haired Lylya asked, "are you feeling better now?"

"Yes, thank you, now off you go."

They kissed his cheeks before slipping off the bed and running from the room.

He reached for his green silk robe painted with grasses as Arno materialised out of nowhere and got to it first. Arno held it out and Kittal slipped into it. Kittal remarked with a smiled to his young servant, "it's good to be home."

He walked through the house that had grown with his family and household. As well as his wife, son and two daughters there were also now several maids to clean and tend to Lulizen and their children. He had Arno, Canaan's replacement, and two secretaries to deal with all the administrative paperwork. Soon there would be two more, another child for them and a tutor for Ozanus. Ozanus was going to find himself busy for the next ten years learning the skills of a Suwar, an armed dragon riding soldier, from Da'ud, and how to be the future Nejus with his father and tutor.

At first he had suggested they move to the empty fortress of Linyee where there was plenty of room for everyone but Lulizen had refused. Although it meant a year of building work he had been relieved she hadn't agreed. For him there were too many bad memories in that place. Instead he had added another floor to his Valley home where the children and servants slept. He still had his bedroom, which he shared with Lulizen, on the ground floor with its light curtains whispering in the breeze coming through all the open windows. The new shingle roof had dragons carved into the ridge of it.

17

Lulizen greeted her husband as he stepped out on to the cool and shady veranda and shooed away the secretary who wanted the Nejus' attention. She smiled warmly at him, admiring him through almond shaped brown eyes full of adoration, "feeling better?"

Though he was twenty years older than her she still didn't regret agreeing to become his wife. His caramel brown hair was becoming greyer, but he was still fit and muscular. His scarred face, scarred by his grandfather's wild dragon, was still handsome with its laughter lines round his eyes though currently they also looked tired.

"Now I am. I have missed you."

She kept him feeling young. Every time he came back to the Valley he was always glad he had joined with her before the villagers and dragons. She had made the Valley alive again like when he and Ciara had been allowed to visit their mother and Titan from Linyee where they had lived with their grandfather.

"You saw me last night." She teased as she rubbed her growing belly. In the last six years she had changed as well, four pregnancies did that. She had grown plumper, but it hadn't stopped him from loving her and in fact she felt sure he loved her even more though she still only reached his shoulder. Her long black hair was still her proudest feature.

"I think I barely noticed last night. It was a long ride back from the border."

"How is Ifor getting on?"

"We are safe from raiders again for the moment. They'll be returning here in the next month to swap over." He smiled grimly. Since Titan had gone his large homeland of Keytel was peaceful but now it was a tempting target for the neighbouring countries and raiders. Titan, as agent to Kittal, had kept the eastlands under control and now there was no one there. It was busier than ever for the Suwars patrolling the borders. Kittal found himself joining the new Suwar Chieftain a lot. At least the island of Jukirla was behaving itself under Tania and Canaan's watchful eye with a squadron of Suwars. A group always lived in the Valley as well now, mainly those with families.

He glanced up at the sky which had dark clouds

lingering in the distance just like they had been for the last few months. Animals and dragons alike had been agitated but he hadn't been able to find a reason. He tried to ignore it but he knew there was something amiss. There had been rain but the humidity was rising. A storm was needed to break the uncomfortable heat. There had been an electric storm but it hadn't broken the heat. The wind whipped up the dust and vegetation with an uncontrolled aggression. He wondered what was going on with the Gods.

Putting a brave face on it he pulled Lulizen to him and asked, "how have you been?"

"This little one is definitely a kicker." She took one of his hands and laid it on her belly. Shyly she suggested, "shall we make sure it is a brother for Ozanus."
Lulizen had shown herself to be very fertile. Lylya had come a year after Ozanus and Shuang had come two years later.

"I like the idea of that. I'll go through the papers tomorrow." He took her hand and together they went down the steps of the veranda to the lawn.

The couple paused on the edge of the lawn as Ozanus, riding Ozi, a young dark red dragon, landed with Da'ud on his dragon. Six-year-old Ozanus grinned at the sight of his parents together. His sun bleached caramel brown hair was his father's but his frame was slight like his mother's for the moment. He slipped from his saddle and ran across the lawn, "next time you go out on Kite can I come? … Sir?"
Kittal looked to Da'ud for confirmation his son was progressing well. The Suwar gave his Nejus a firm nod.

"We will see Ozanus."
Ozanus smiled a smile of adoration at his father and then turned to his dragon who was twice his size, *"did you hear that? Next time we will be going out with father."* He was still learning how to speak the dragon's tongue but was showing he was his father's son in how quickly he was picking it up.

"Come on." Lulizen tugged at Kittal.
He turned from his son who was now helping Da'ud get the saddle off Ozi and allowed Lulizen to draw him deeper into the valley, through the lush vegetation. The valley with its hot pools
19

that kept it warm all year round was surrounded by grey cliffs, spotted with green vegetation and dragon nests.

Coming upon the Pool of Heirs they stopped. The clear waters overhung with willows and edged with tall reeds looked inviting in the heat of the strange day. Kittal helped Lulizen out of her two silk robes which were tied in place with a sash above her bump. After Ozanus she found it easier to wear clothes in the style of her court when pregnant. He stripped as well and dived into the sun warmed water from the bank.

He came up for air laughing and beckoned Lulizen into the water. She carefully lowered herself in. She swam towards him and he wrapped his arms round her as they treaded water.

They finally allowed themselves to submit to the lust they were both feeling. They kissed hard and passionately as they tread water. She closed her eyes and moaned as his hands moved over her swollen breasts and stomach and then down between her thighs. She could feel his erection pressing between her buttocks and rubbed herself against it, teasing him. She giggled as she heard him moan. He wanted her so badly now.

They began to swim towards the bank.

Suddenly Kittal wasn't with her. She turned and couldn't spot him. She smiled ready for him to appear and surprise her. The smile turned to worry as he didn't appear. She ducked underwater trying to see him but he seemed to have vanished. She rose and gulped a lungful of air before ducking under again. She spun slowly on the spot looking down. Nothing.

The water became chilly and deadly. Fighting tears she swam to the edge and pulled herself out and wrapped her two robes around herself.

Kittal had been looking forward to getting out of the water and taking Lulizen. He had impatiently waited till the moment she wanted sex again and now…

One moment he had been on the surface with his young wife and the next he was being pulled down. Looking down he saw nothing and realised the pool had become a bottomless abyss. Looking up the surface had disappeared. A part of him wanted to fight what was happening but a calmness descended

20

over him. He came to realise he was no longer in the Pool of Heirs.

A voice came out of the swirling currents, *"I need your help Nejus."*

"Lord?" Kittal called out.
A golden claw came out of a current followed by the nostrils of a dragon's snout and then both disappeared again.

"One of my sons was missing. Recently he has been spotted." Kittal saw the glowing scaly side of a God. The end of its tail flicked the currents towards him, spinning him. He called out as he tried to spot the God again, *"how?"*

"He is not strong enough to return to us and seems to have forgotten who he is. You must go to him and bring him back to the Valley. You must get him back to us."

"But I don't know where he is or what he looks like." Kittal protested.

"You must travel across the Sea of Cenfornr. Find him before they realise what he is."

"I have a country to run and family to protect."

"I will watch over them." The tail flashed past again and Kittal felt the power of the God emitting from it, *"you have the strength and powers of the High Priest to protect him and then get him back to us. Do not fail me."* The God threatened at the end.

"How will I know it is him?"

"You are not worthy of my gifts if you don't recognise him." The voice scoffed leaving Kittal worried and hoping he would be able to identify this lost God.

"Yes my Lord." Kittal attempted to bow in the ethereal waters.

"Go now." The Dragon God brushed past, spinning Kittal again.

He started to ascend in a whirling mass of bubbles and exploded out of the water. He fell heavily back into the water with a large splash, stunning him. He bobbed back to the surface and floated for a moment before beginning to sink.

Seeing him Lulizen cried out, "no!"
She threw off her robes and ran for the water. She slid into the

21

water and swam for her husband. She grabbed his arm. She felt a surge of energy go up her arm giving her the strength she needed to pull Kittal to the bank.

She flopped beside his still body gasping for breath and weeping. The weeping became a laugh of relief as he coughed and rolled over and coughed up a lungful of water. He groaned and tried to get up.

"What happened to you? Don't scare me like that ever again." Lulizen exclaimed, hitting him in the shoulder.

He slowly opened his eyes, "the Gods…." He put a hand to his head and let out a long moan, "Oooh, my head."

"Kittal?!" She tried to get his attention.

He turned to look at her and for a moment thought he was still with the Gods as she was haloed by the late afternoon sun. He asked carefully, "where am I?"

She frowned, "your valley home in Keytel."

He breathed a sigh of relief.

"What has just happened Kittal? You disappeared." She helped him sit up and put his robe round him. All desire for sex had dissipated and been replaced with concern. He still looked a little confused.

He blinked and his eyes began to focus, "Lulizen?"

She smiled softly, "yes."

"I was with the Dragon Lord. There is a God missing and he wants me to find him." He looked at his young wife with fear, "and I'm not allow to fail."

"What does that mean?" She asked.

"I have to die trying." He remarked solemnly.

"But you've only just got back." She protested, "what about me and the children? And Keytel?"

"I will have to you leave you as regent. This isn't going to be a week or two. I have no idea how long I'm going to be away." He drew her to him.

"What about the little one?"

He took a deep breath, "I don't think I can delay."

She fought back tears as he wrapped his strong arms round her. She didn't want to have to rule Keytel in his place. It was too much responsibility. Since she had been with him he had never

22

been away longer than a few weeks. He had never asked her to act as regent as he hadn't needed to. She hadn't been trained to rule even as regent. She hadn't even tried to learn from her husband as she didn't think she would never need to.

It was a sombre dinner that evening. The children usually chatted or squabbled but tonight they behaved, sensing something amiss. They saw their parents sitting so close they were almost like one person. Shuang began crying as she didn't like the atmosphere and the children's nurse took her away. Ozanus and Lylya glanced at each other and then at their parents but as they didn't fully understand and their father's expression deterred them they didn't ask questions.

Lulizen clung to her husband. She didn't know when she would next be sharing their bed with him. She didn't know if she would even see him again. And then there was their unborn child, would it know its father?

It was with urgency and an attempt to stretch the night out that they made love that night. Lulizen moaned and sighed under Kittal's touch. Every time she thought she couldn't take any more he would retreat and find another spot to turn her into a quivering wreck. By the time he took her from behind while they lay on their sides she felt like liquid and that they were melting together. They sighed together, their desire finally sated.

The tension from the previous night that all the servants could sense lifted. They knew something was going on but only a teenaged blonde curly haired Arno knew what. They moved quietly around the house in the morning so as not to disturb their Nejus and Nejusana until Arno and Rafferty, one of Kittal's secretaries were sent for.

Lulizen lay under the sheets dozing while Kittal moved around the bedroom and then into his study followed by the two servants. He spun round, surprising both men, "I am having to go away."

"Kite is ready when you are sir." Arno said as he disappeared to pack the Nejus' saddlebags. He had taken well to being Kittal's new man servant and had quickly learnt everything considering his age.

"I will travel light." Kittal called after the young man. He turned to Rafferty, a tall thin man with a thin genial face well suited to life as a secretary with good inkmanship, "we need to write up two documents."

"Sir?"

"An announcement and a will. I haven't got the time to wait for everyone to get here." Kittal sat down at his desk and began dictating.

The declaration and will took most of the morning to write. It was with reluctance that he wrote his will, putting plans in place to support both his wife and his eldest child. At six years old his son knew nothing of ruling. He kept his back to the secretary as he dictated. He wanted no one to see his agony. Ozanus was in a worse position then himself. At least he had had his grandfather to prepare him; Ozanus had only him and if he died…. He didn't want to think about that.

Lulizen watched as he dressed to go flying, putting on his pale grey padded jacket with a skirt over shirt and trousers and boots. He adjusted the sleeve where the tight lower half had twisted. He tucked his dragon-hide gloves into his belt. They were not actually made of dragon skin but thick flexible leather. Also tucked into his belt was his dragon headed knife and his sabre also hung from it. He loosely wrapped the headscarf round his head as he gave his wife a tight smile. Silently he held out a hand and she took it.

She took several deep breaths as she was led from the house to the veranda where the villagers that supplied Kittal's household and the Suwars were gathered along with a few curious dragons. Ozanus ran out in his own flying clothes, a similar shade of dark red to Ozi, crying out happily, "are we going out papa?"

The boy stumbled to a stop and stared at the gathering and his parents. He frowned, "what is going on?"

Kittal crouched and picked his son up, "something very important."

"Can I come with you?"

24

"No. I need you to stay with your mama. Where I am going is not for a child."

Ozanus pouted, not fully understanding.

Kittal turned to the audience, "the Dragon Lord has given me a task to do. I must seek out a God who has fallen from the heavens."

The audience murmured to each other in shock. Kittal continued, "I do not know how long I will be gone so I leave Keytel in my wife's capable hands with a selection of advisors. I leave yourselves under her care in return you will protect your Nejusana and our children."

The Suwars bowed and saluted, fists pressed to their chests.

They parted to allow Kittal and Lulizen though. Deigo and Joli, a blue tinted dragon with coastal ancestry, stood at a discreet distance from Kite, a grey dragon that was Kittal's own ride, who had been saddled earlier by Arno. She leant forward on the pair of large claws that were on a joint of her large wings. Ozanus wiggled in his father's hold until Kittal put him down. Angry that he wasn't going to be flying with his father he ran back to the house. Kittal opened his mouth to call his son back but Lulizen stopped him, "I'll talk to him later."

He nodded and asked, "you'll be alright won't you?"

"I will. Get word to me if you can. Have you got that new tonic for Tania?"

Though Kittal had healed his daughter's broken bones it seemed he hadn't fully healed her body. Lulizen quite often felt guilty when she heard Tania had miscarried again while hers and Kittal's family grew.

"Yes." Kittal said distractedly as he checked all the straps and buckles of his saddle and saddlebags and that his bow and quiver of arrows were secure. He wouldn't admit it but it was hard to have to leave Lulizen so soon after getting back.

She knew and softly said, "come here." She beckoned him to her.

He crossed to her and she took hold of his chin and drew his face down to hers. She whispered so the dragons and Diego wouldn't hear, "you must obey your Gods no matter how much I want to keep you here. Just remember you are my everything and our

25

love will get us through anything. Come back safe so this little one knows his father." She kissed him then, hard on the lips while trying not to cling to him.

"I won't promise anything but not even an angry God will stop me from trying." He said solemnly. He called over to Diego, "time to go."

"Yes sir." Diego, a well built brown haired, brown eyed young man who had plenty of women fluttering their eyes at him, grinned as he climbed on to Joli unassisted. He no longer needed his crutches as Kittal had partly fixed his broken twisted leg once he had discovered he could heal bones after he had healed his daughter's broken back. He still walked with a limb but he more than made up for as a competent Suwar.

Lulizen stepped back as Kittal climbed up on to Kite, climbing up via her claws. With a sigh he remarked, *"time to go old girl."*

"A little less of the old girl." She retorted, *"are you going to tell me what's going on now? Arno just said you have been set a mission by our overlord."*

"It's true." He answered as Kite rose into the air and she waved down at Lulizen who waved sorrowfully back, *"we head to Jukirla."*

Joli and Kite rose high into the air with their riders. Joli and Deigo kept a discreet distance back from their Nejus. Though Kittal could handle most situations on his own he knew he got no younger so appreciated having Deigo as a companion when flying around Keytel. As for Diego he was proud to be his Nejus' personal guard and together they had got out of a few scraps that Lulizen didn't get to know about.

Ahead of him and Joli, Kittal and Kite talked, *"so what must we do?"*

"One of our Gods has fallen from the heavens and I have to find him though I don't know how. Do you know of such an occurrence happening in your collective memories?"

"Not that I'm aware of but this is a big world and it may have happened somewhere else and not reached us."

"I had a feeling you would say that. If we find this God do you think you would recognise it?"

26

"I don't know. Did our noble Lord give any idea of where he might be?"

"Across the Sea of Cenfornr."

"Oh?" Kite remarked with surprise.

"Do you know if there are any dragons over there?"
She shook her head, *"no, sorry. Maybe some of the island dragons know. I know a few have explored further afield, or maybe the sea serpents."*

"Mmm."

"What if we don't find him?" She asked with fear.
Kittal gulped back his personal concerns, *"then I'm not worthy. It might be that I will have to spent the rest of my life seeking this God."*

"I'll go wherever you go." She remarked thinking similar thoughts as Kittal, would she ever get to see Lupe and her daughter again?

"Thank you. Let us pray it doesn't come to that." Kittal turned to their companions, "we'll camp out tonight and hopefully reach Jukirla tomorrow."

"Yes sir. I can see a good spot ahead." Diego shouted back after pulling down his turban from his mouth.

"That'll do then."

All four of them were quiet as they sat round the fire. Diego leant against Joli wrapped in a blanket already asleep. Kittal sat with Kite's tail protectively around him. Balanced between his crossed legs was a bowl of water. He dipped a hand into it and then out with barely a ripple. The surface misted over and then cleared to reveal Lulizen kissing their three children as they fell asleep. She turned and looked around as if she sensed a presence. She smiled knowingly to herself and pressed fingertips to her lips. Kittal smiled himself, she knew he was looking on.

With a heavy sigh he poured the water from the bowl. He needed to meditate and hope more information came forth to help him with his task. He settled himself, drew in and released a few deep breaths to calm himself and closed his eyes and shut away all mundane thoughts.

He drifted into a mind of mistiness and he could sense

27

confusion and also immense power that had been forgotten. He looked round but it was too gloomy to see anything. Suddenly there was light and he was looking into a stone walled room with a young man and woman in it. Kittal was drawn to the young man and realised he had briefly been in his mind. The young man was so pale he looked like he was nearly dead. His skin was tinged an ashen grey and he wondered how the woman in a worn yellow dress didn't see it. The young man sat up and stared directly at Kittal with stern reptilian eyes. Kittal stared right back, this was who he needed to find. He held up a hand, palm facing the man. He let the healing powers flow through him towards the god who had forgotten he was one.

The man's back arched and he cried out. The young woman fell to the floor and covered herself with her hands with a cry of her own. She covered her head as she saw him stretch and change, a tail whipping round….

Four

Myrskyr saw the man standing in the corner of the room. He had felt the man's presence in his mind before he had materialised. He stared at the man with the scarred cheek and greying hair and recognised a fellow being who had once been a prisoner but there was more than that to him. He sensed that he was familiar; not that he had known him personally but that he had always been aware of him and that he was important. He saw the man rise a hand and felt himself begin to change.

His back arched and he cried out in pain, what was happening to him? He watched wide eyed as his body stretched and grew, the clothes on his body stretching and ripping. He saw Zhina fling herself to the floor and cover her head to protect herself.

He grew to fill the room, a long dark purple scaled body and tail curled round the walls to be able to fit. Hands turned to claws before his eyes and racked down the stonewalls leaving four parallel gouged lines. He roared and flexed new muscles. He cried out in his mind, *"what am I?!"*
He looked to the man that hadn't moved or flinched as he had become a dragon. He demanded, *"who are you?!"*
Before the man could answer the grey eyes of the man rolled into the back of his head and Myrskyr began to shrink into a human form again.

Myrskyr rolled off the bed, naked and landed on the floor breathing heavily. He sought the man in the corner, wanting him to be still there but he wasn't. He looked to Zhina who still cowered on the floor whimpering with her hands over her ears from the deep reptilian roar.

He reached out to her. Slowly she opened her eyes and removed her hands from her ears. He asked, "did you see him?"

"See who? Myrskyr, do you know what just happened?"

He frowned, "what?"

"You just turned into a huge dragon."

"I did?" He lifted himself up and gazed round the room. Most of the furniture was turned over. The jug had fallen and broken on the floor. The sheets from his bed were ripped and there were several scratches in groups of four on the walls.

Zhina sat back on her knees and gazed round herself. If the Empress found out she had no idea what would happen but one thing was certain Myrskyr would become even more of a prisoner then he already was. If she could delay that she would. She got to her feet and ordered, "help me get this place back to normal and put some clothes on."

Deep within the palace Empress Esperanza sat up, startling the maids who slept at the foot of the bed. She was alert. She had heard a roar followed by a clap of thunder. She demanded, "my robe."

Once in a warm robe she hurried through the lamp lit palace with a stomach twisting with excitement, had it finally happened? She found the guard cowering opposite the door, shaking hands pointing a spear at the locked iron braced wooden door. She ordered, "unlock that door now."

"Majesty…." The man shakily said. He fumbled the key but finally got it in and unlocked the door.

Neither knew what to expect as the guard opened the door and peered round. Everything looked normal with the two occupants apparently asleep though the sheets looked a bit ragged. She stepped into the room and looked round as the occupants sat up, sensing her presence.

The Empress' eyes were drawn to the deep scratches on the wall. Excitement and anger fleetingly appeared on her face before she became her emotionless self again. Why would he not reveal himself to her? She drew her hand down the scratches and looked down. Myrskyr looked back at her nervously. She tried to remain calm though frustration accented her voice, "why will you not reveal yourself Lord? I don't want to harm you, I want to

30

work with you. Together we can make Sunulanda a great, strong and powerful country. Is that not why you came?”

"I'm not a god.” He protested and he was not pretending. He didn't know what she was talking about.

“Yes you are!” She exclaimed, “you can't hide from me forever.” She turned to the guard, “chain him to the wall. He's not escaping.” Back at Myrskyr she declared, “you will reveal yourself.”
She stalked out of the room leaving Zhina and the guard staring at Myrskyr.

He looked back at them with confusion. He was beginning to wonder if there was something wrong with him as he had seen a man Zhina hadn't and she claimed he had become a dragon. Something had definitely happened, but he didn't know what.

Five

Joli and Kite glanced at each other with worry as Kittal dropped to the ground from where his meditating had caused him to levitate. He landed with a groan. Kite cautiously asked, *"Nejus?"*

Kittal looked up and with a maniac laugh said, *"I found him!"* He sobered up and added, *"though I still don't know where."* Joli and Kite stared at Kittal, wondering if the stress of potential failure had unhinged their Nejus.

"Are you sure?" Kite tentatively asked, *"should our Lord have given you this task?"*

He replied, *"I'm fine. I didn't think I would find him while meditating. I now know I **will** be able to find him."*

"What does he look like?" Joli couldn't help being curious.

"Like the mountain dragons and is a dark purple which would suggest he is a Storm God."

"They can be quite vicious. We'll have to be careful around him. We won't want him angry." Kite remarked.

"We'll need to find him first." Kittal pointed out, *"now, I should probably try and get some sleep."*

Attempting to heal the God had drained him but thoughts ran through his mind. He had never thought that he would find himself healing a god and he hadn't been strong enough this time. The only reason he could think of was that he was still weary from fighting the raiders and the flight home. It was going to be at least a week before he felt strong enough to try again.

He dozed in his saddle as they flew on to Jukirla. Joli

and Diego flew alongside Kite keeping an eye on their Nejus slumped on Kite's back. Diego asked, *"what happened last night? Is he all right?"*

"He found the god while meditating." Joli answered.

"That's good isn't it?" Diego had heard the worry in Joli's voice.

"Yes but we still have no idea where he is and it seems the god might be a Storm God."

"Oh...."

They fell into silence as they flew over green fields and forests towards the coast and Senspanta and then over the sea to Jukirla. Below them Senspanta was as rough looking as when Kittal had travelled through nine years previous. Though it was rough there were plenty of men with astute business heads who did a deal with Kittal to enable them to become a freeport.

They landed in the forest clearing of the Smythman estate where Bonn and Katrine greeted them with reserve. Bonn had never completely forgiven Kittal for releasing all the dragons. Then there was the fact Arno had gone to the valley as a soldier and then stayed to become a servant to the man. Aware of the family's feelings Kittal said, "we will not demand anything. We will be gone by first light."
Bonn asked stiffly, "how is Arno?"

"He is well. He asked me to pass this on to you." From a saddlebag Kittal pulled out a sealed letter and held it out for Katrine to take.

"Thank you." Katrine took it and then retreated to stand beside Bonn while the two men and dragons headed to the far end of the clearing.

True to their word they were gone from the clearing with the first rays of dawn turning the sky orange. Below them the quarries and mines were still worked but now horses pulled the raw materials around the island. Only a few dragons remained on the island, staying well away from man. Though they were free they didn't trust the Jukirlans not to abuse them again.

A year after Kittal had taken control of Jukirla and cut the Governor's head off his son, Dunan, had led a small rebellion

33

killing several Suwars and two dragons. Kittal had retaliated as promised and all involved had died; executed with a hail of arrows from the surviving Suwars. With the leaders dead the rest were sent to the mines for five years.

Now it was peaceful with Tania and Canaan governing the island. It had proven to be a wise choice as the islanders had taken the young couple to their hearts and with a few adjustments the island had begun to prosper again.

The port of Jukir hadn't changed much either with the heavy industries and warehouses down at the docks and the houses becoming wealthier and larger up the hill towards the Governor's House. The houses with long gardens behind them were squashed together but rose up three or four storeys high with large windows and tall roofs. The position of the Governor's House gave it a perfect view of the docks and whole town so nothing could be missed as traders and ships came and went.

Kite and Joli landed in the Suwars' barracks courtyard, constructed behind the Governor's House to house the Suwars. The dirt surface was large enough to allow two dragons to land while the roof of the barracks was strengthened to allow dragons to perch on it. A Suwar ran forward from his guard post, "Nejus, we weren't expecting you."

"Something at short notice has come up." Kittal remarked as he slipped from Kite's back.

"Your daughter will be happy to see you."

"Thank you." Kittal headed towards the Governor's House enclosed by a brick wall leaving Diego and the Suwar to unsaddle the dragons. It didn't take long for them both to start updating each other on their separate lives.

Tania sat in the immaculate garden behind the house in a rose arbour wrapped in a shawl against the cool morning air. Around her the garden was laid out around plots of flowers bordered by small hedges. Trees overhung one corner where there was a round bench covered in cushions. She looked forward to the mornings before the nausea came and everyone started fussing over her, apart from Canaan. He had withdrawn

34

from her, having now given up hoping they might have a child of their own.

She looked up as she heard footsteps and was surprised to see her father coming towards her, running his hands over the budding lavender. She managed a brief smile as she rubbed her slightly swollen stomach.

He came and sat beside her on the bench concerned by how pale and tired she was with bruising under her eyes. She looked so much older than her thirty years with her normal shiny caramel brown hair looking lanky. Tania asked, "what are you doing here father though it's nice to have you."

"The Dragon Lord has set me a task."

"Oh?"

"But that can wait. Are you….?"

She sadly nodded, "it's fighting to stay with me but it's leaving me so tired..." Her voice failed her as she let her father envelope her in his arms. The tears fell from brown eyes.

"I have prayed to the Gods…." And clearly their mind was on their own kind, "but I have another herbal infusion for you which might help."

"You look like you need some yourself." She softly remarked as she broke out of his arms.

"I'll be all right." He had realised a long time ago that the one disadvantage to having the powers within him was he was left feeling tired if he used a large amount in one go and it took him a while to recover each time.

They both looked up as they heard footsteps on the gravel path. Canaan came towards them carrying a tray with a pot of hot water and two cups on it. Dressed in a brown coat edged discreetly in a dark brown on the cuffs and collar over a linen shirt and with his short blonde hair he looked well suited to the islanders' clothes.

Canaan briefly looked suspicious until he recognised his father-by-marriage. He exclaimed, "sir? We weren't expecting you. When did you arrive?"

"On the island last night, here, about an hour ago."

"Where did you stay?"

"At Bonn Symthman's. I wanted to fly over the island and

check all was well.”

“You do know they complain every time.” Tania sighed.

“I can set down wherever I want.” Kittal remarked sternly, “I had a letter from Arno for them. They should be grateful that their son wasn't killed and that he is doing well as my servant.”

“There must be a reason for being here?” Canaan eyed his Nejus as he poured the hot water into a cup containing a herbal infusion and handed it over to Tania.

Now was one of the few times in a day they got to themselves, before the pregnancy dominated Tania's mind and body again; and he had the duties of being Governor.

“Father has brought a new infusion for us to try.” Tania remarked with a tight smile as she sipped the old infusion, “but he has also been given a task by the Dragon Lord.”

“Oh?”

“There is a God missing somewhere in this world and it’s not in Keytel. I was told he is somewhere across the Sea of Confernr. You haven't heard anything from any traders?”

Canaan looked thoughtful for a moment. Jukirla and Senspanta received a lot of travellers from across the sea but he had heard nothing about any god or dragon, “I've heard nothing…..
though…. There is a queen over there who is fanatical about the gods. There is a story of a man falling from the sky during a storm.”

“Where is this?”

“Come, I'll show you on a map.” Canaan stood and beckoned his Nejus.

Kittal frowned with concern. Apart from one brief loving look Canaan had barely acknowledge Tania's presence. He knew they were struggling with the pregnancies but was their love for each other fading? As he followed Canaan out of the garden and into the house he challenged the young man, “what's going on between the two of you?”

Canaan glanced at Kittal at his side. He didn't want to really talk about what was going on between himself and Tania. He didn't want any more pity. He took a deep breath before saying, “I still love her but I can't spend my time hoping for it not to happen anymore. I have this island to look after… We've had four

36

miscarriages.”

There were unspoken memories behind those words that both men knew of. There were was a fifth that Canaan didn't speak of. The first loss had been when Tania fell from the walls of Titan's castle.

“I can't keep watching her put herself through this. It's destroying her. Every time she hopes so desperately and then crumbles when she fails. Is there nothing you can do so she can never have another pregnancy?” Canaan looked to Kittal, silently pleading with him.

Kittal felt torn. He wanted Tania to have the child she wanted but he wanted her fit and well and happy again. He wanted Tania and Canaan to be happy as a couple again as well. Together they were stronger though Canaan had shown himself to be a proficient ruler with Hamin by his side.

“I will speak with her once we know which way this pregnancy goes.” Kittal answered finally, fighting to keep his voice emotionless. Often he was stern but he couldn't be with his children. He adored all of them too much to be unemotional and distant.

Once in the Governor House's library Canaan pulled out a large map which had the coastline of Keytel with the port city of Senspanta and the island Jukirla to the right hand edge. Stretching across most of the map was the Sea of Confernr with sea dragons painted on it. In the bottom, off centre was Sunulanda. There was a scattering of towns along the coastline and behind them was forest with roads streaking through. Towards the bottom corner was a thick line marking a country boundary. On the bottom edge was marked a city, “that is Bakamon where the queen lives. She styles herself Empress. I think you might have to try there first.”

As Kittal studied the map he asked, “how long is the journey?”

“About a week by sail, maybe longer depending on the weather and sometimes not at all if a dragon attacks.”

“There are no islands at all so I'm not going to be able to fly with Kite.” Kittal frowned, “mmm… When's the next ship?”

“Not for a while. One left in that direction yesterday.”

"I know the sea dragons are quite wild but I'll have to see if one might take me." Kittal remarked thoughtfully.

"There's a pod of them that passes by most evenings. I've discovered they love to show off. They jump out of the waters."

"Thanks Canaan. Where's the best place to see them?"

"Lets all go this evening." Canaan suggested as he began to roll up the map.

"That sounds like an excellent idea."

"So what God has supposedly fallen out of the Heavens?"

"I saw him while meditating. I tried healing him but didn't have enough strength to do it from so far away. I think he's a storm god."

"Do you know, we had a storm the other day but the thunder was missing from it. The dragons were all quite restless afterwards, afraid…." Canaan contemplated.

"So it seems I'm seeking the Thunder God."

"Perhaps."

"I might go see them later and see if they know anything else. Now, when is breakfast served?"

"The Suwars have the better breakfast if you want to head back to the barracks. I have a meeting this morning and Tania will be pulling toast to pieces in an attempt to eat it." Canaan remarked with embarrassment, "if I'd…"
Kittal waved the ending away, "don't worry. I'll head to the barracks."

Returning to the barracks breakfast had just been set out. The Suwars were all young men and women with no families of their own to tie them close to home. They stood as Kittal entered and saluted, fists against chests. Hamin stepped away from his chair at the head of the long table and made way for his High Chieftain, "sir, it is an honour as always to have you here."
The right-hand side of the table shuffled down the bench so their commander could sit down. Diego had squeezed himself in on the left hand side and with several others had already started getting food for himself. Hamin cleared his throat and everyone stopped. Hamin picked up his clay cup of tea and stood, "may the Gods continue to bless our Nejus with good health and peace. May he have another healthy child."

38

"Here, here!" The others called out.

"And may he have a successful mission. I think I can speak for all of us that we would willingly come with you."

"And I would love your support but sadly I can't take you. I have to go across the Sea of Confernr and no dragon can fly that far without resting." Kittal remarked as he gestured for everyone to start eating.

Plates of bread, bacon, eggs and cheese were passed round. Bowls of spelt cooked in sweet milk were shared out from a large pot. Pots of herbal infused tea steamed as everyone tucked in and started talking.

Hamin looked on with pride at all his young Suwars. All were capable men and women and were great assets to the tribe. He leant towards Kittal, "how do you plan to get across then?"

"I am not sure though have a possible idea. Canaan mentioned something earlier. What did the dragons say when there was no thunder?"

"They fear that the world would come to an end. No thunder during a storm is very rare as it tends to herald the arrival of a normal much welcomed reprieve in the weather. The weather at the moment is… is off. Can you tell me anymore that I can pass on to them?" Hamin glanced down the table but no one was paying the two old men any attention.

"Just that I will not let the world end. A God is lost and I will find him."

"I will reassure them."

"Thank you Hamin. It seems that it is more urgent then ever if we are to keep the wild ones calm. If they get agitated I will not be able to stop them from being dangerous to man and beast." Kittal frowned with worry.

"We'll do our best. At least our dragons are not too afraid though they are worried."

Kittal spent the rest of the day down in the old town of Jukir getting as much information as possible on Sunulanda. He found that Empress Esperanza was obsessed with the Gods. She was a little crazed in the head and believed a young man that had fallen through the ceiling during a storm was a god. No one

39

could tell Kittal what he looked like as she kept him locked in the palace with her.

As for the country itself a lot of it was forested and wild. Few ventured off the roads for fear of being eaten by wild animals though no one could say what they were. It was a country of two halves. The Sunulandas were excellent farmers and winemakers and craftsmen but they also lived in fear, their lives dictated by the Gods and their Empress, and their superstitions. Only a few were allow to leave the country to trade by land and sea and they didn't like strangers.

Kittal realised it was going to be just as hard to find the god once in Sunulanda as it was going to be getting there. He would have to travel carefully so as not to be stopped and arrested. And then he was going to have to get into the palace.

It was with a heavy heart he returned to the top of the town for dinner with Canaan and Tania. It was quiet and tense as the two men watched Tania play with her food. She knew she should eat but the smell of the food just turned her stomach. She was living on her father's infusions and dry biscuits and a meat broth that was more water than meat.

Sensing her father watching she looked up and smiled tentatively and lifted a forkful of green beans to her mouth. Before eating she remarked, "Canaan told me what our plans are tonight. It is a sight to see especially as there is still enough moonlight to see by."

"Eat so you are strong enough to come." Canaan said sternly without looking at his wife.

Tania glanced at him, her head bowed in shame that her father had to see how far apart she and Canaan had become. She wondered if he would let her return to the family home but then she didn't want to. Lulizen wouldn't purposely do it but it would feel like she was showing off her fertility with her younger half brother and sisters. She felt sure her father would be disappointed as well. She gulped down the green beans. She would give her father his first grandchild even if it killed her.

It was with relief that dinner ended and with Hamin and Diego they headed to the cliffs holding lanterns to help them up the path. They stood making small talk under the light of the half

40

moon waiting for the pod of sea dragons.

There was a swelling of the surface as the bodies of six dragons displaced the water underneath. Three were full grown eel like dragons with flat tails and large iridescence green scales. A double row of finlets ran down their backs. They rose out of the water, arching their slender muscular bodies. They snorted water out of their nostrils before descending again with barely a ripple.

The three youngsters weren't quite so controlled. They leapt into the air, twisting their bodies and letting out a roar. They dropped back into the waves with huge splashes and circled each other to then rise up again. They moved out of the way as the three adults returned from the depths. They rose higher than the three young ones and then crashed back into the sea.

Canaan remarked to Kittal, "they love showing off but I don't think they'll talk to you."
Kittal looked thoughtful and then a smile formed. He was definitely too old for craziness but if it would get the sea dragons' attention and impress them enough to listen he would do it. He pulled off his tunic and boots and handed them to Diego along with his knife. Tania exclaimed, "what are you doing?!"

"Going to impress some dragons into giving me a ride." Adrenalin was rushing through his blood now. The things he did for the Gods, dragons and his family.

"Can't you wait for a ship?"

"No. Meet me down at the quays Diego."

"Sir?" Diego wasn't sure about this.

"Wish me luck." Kittal called out as he began running towards the edge of the cliffs. He leapt as far out as possible to hopefully miss the waves crashing against the shore. He adjusted the shape of his body so he dove into the water clasped hands first.

Six

He flew through the water till his momentum slowed. He hung in the water a moment before starting to kick his way to the surface. A young sea dragon loomed into view, *"wow, that was impressive."*

"Thank you."

"I've never seen a human do that before."

"Who are you?" Another appeared and circled Kittal suspiciously.

"I am known to many dragons as the Nejus." Kittal carefully answered, *"I am seeking assistance. Who leads your group?"*

"That is Ocranii." The first spoke. She headed towards the surface and Kittal followed.

Breaking the surface he looked round. He heard shouts from the cliff top and shouted up, "I'm fine."
Though his body would probably ache in the morning. After a few deep breathes he ducked back down, glad he had the powers of the gods to allow him to breath underwater. He called out, *"noble lords, I seek Ocranii."*
One of the adults appeared, scars from chains criss-crossing its body and long snout. It demanded as it swam past, trying to unnerve the man, *"what do you want man?"*

"One of the Lords of the Sky is missing and I have been sent by our shared Overlord to find him."

"I heard a rumour, so it is true." Ocranii reappeared and stopped in front of Kittal, *"you are the Nejus? You helped free us?"*

"I did."

"You have been given the powers of the Gods." Ocranii stated

"Yes."

"Then I suppose I should be grateful." Ocranii glared.

"I do not come seeking recognition for my deeds. I come seeking help."

"What sort?"

"I must travel across the Sea of Confernr quickly. I can't fly as I normally would. I come to ask if you or one of your kin will take me across."

The dragon swam off and Kittal thought the answer was no. It had been worth a try.

Taking Kittal by surprise another adult rose up from underneath him and he found himself straddling the back of her. She turned, *"ready to go?"*

"Err...."

"Go now or not at all." Ocranii said sharply, reappearing alongside Kittal, *"the sooner you find the missing god the less likely the world will descend into chaos."*

"Can we pass by the quay to let someone know and let me get my knife?"

"No." Ocranii snarled.

"Of course." Kittal's ride responded and snapped at Ocranii.

"Thank you....?"

"Tun. It is an honour to help our Nejus. Ignore him, he's always grumpy."

"Hmpfh." Ocranii swam off again.

Tun swam round the island to Jukir's quays. She stopped at a distance where a net would not reach and surfaced, *"I'm going no closer."*

"I'll be back in ten minutes." Kittal said as he slipped off.

Reaching the quay he clung to a rope looped between iron rings as Diego knelt down, placing a lantern beside him. Diego held out a hand, "grab hold sir and I'll pull you up." Breathing heavily Kittal answered, "I'm not getting out. It's now or not at all."

"Oh?"

"It is too far for our own to fly as there is nowhere to pause and rest when I looked at the map, not even a sandbank. I was going to tell you once I found out if the sea dragons would take me.

43

Can you pass me my knife and pouch?"

"I should be coming with you." Diego protested.

"I'm sorry. Stay here on Jukirla and wait for me."
Diego fetched Kittal's dragon headed knife and pouch of money,
"for how long for?"

"I don't know. Please give my apologies to Canaan, Tania and
Kite." Kittal took the knife and pouch.

"If you aren't back in six months I'm coming to find you."

"Don't promise anything you will regret." Kittal said sternly as
he pushed away from the stone quay to return to Tun.
Diego stood and watched his lord and master swim away. To
himself he murmured, "may the gods protect you."

Kittal swam back to the dragon who silently circled
beneath the waves. Ducking down to find her he said, *"I am
ready."*

"Get back on my back and hold tight."
Kittal swam on and held tight to a finlet as Tun turned and
headed out to sea. He glanced back at the rapidly disappearing
ship hulls and wondered if he would ever return.

It wasn't easy riding the dragon especially when she
went chasing after fish. There were many times when he felt
himself losing his grip and being pulled away by the dragon's
watery slipstream. He had to call out a few times to get Tun to
slow down so he could adjust his hold. He would pull himself
further up the body ready to gradually slip back down again.

Above them the waves rose as a storm brewed, the wind
catching at the tops. Tun rose up the surface for them to breath
some fresh salty air. Kittal remarked, *"we shouldn't stay up here
long."*
Ahead of them was a wall of rain. Around them the wind
whipped up the waves over their heads, showering them with
spray. Tun looked to the sky and its black clouds, *"the Gods are
restless. There is no thunder to warn us of a coming storm."*

*"I believe it is the Thunder God I seek. Let's get below where
the storm can't harm us."*

"How could he fall from the heavens?" Tun asked as she and
Kittal dipped below the waves.

44

Sleep finally caught up with him. His hold on the dragon loosened and he began sinking as Tun carried on without realising she had lost her passenger. Feeling the chill and the pressure in his ears he woke. He felt too tired to try and swim back to the surface. Fear caught at his heart, never would he see his home and family again. He had tried and failed.

He felt something sweep pass him. His body wanted nothing more than to die but his mind became alert. A golden glow came towards him becoming so bright that he had to squint. The glow formed into a golden scaled dragon with a long head and body. Four clawed legs lay against its side as it swam towards Kittal, *"you are not going to die, you still have work to do."*
The mouth opened wide and Kittal thought he was about to be swallowed whole.

At the last moment the crested head twisted so that it caught Kittal to push him towards the surface. The mouth didn't close though it could easily have bitten him in half.

Kittal closed his eyes, feeling strangely safe. He was aware of a dense aura of power surrounding the golden dragon and at this moment it was urging him to just sleep.

His mind was carried up to the heavens, through the layer of black clouds. Two dragons came into view, one iridescent purple with a horn on it's nose with a static spark on its point and the other a darker purple and hornless. They charged at each other and as the first snapped at the other, lightning streaked from it. The dark purple one retreated and roared and the sound of thunder boomed so loud Kittal wanted to cover his ears. The pair charged at each other again. The Lightning God lifted a four toed claw and slashed the back of the Thunder God. The Thunder God stumbled away and fell. A third dragon appeared, black as the storm clouds. With its tail it swept a hole in the clouds and the Thunder God fell through it. A voice said, *"they always fight, but this felt different. My sister briefly spotted him before his brother covered her sight with his clouds. That is how I know he is in Bakamon. He doesn't know who he is. He's so far away from himself even I can't reach him but you have managed to. I sensed it."*

Seven

As the sun warmed the sand Kittal stirred. He rolled on to his back and his eyes slowly focused on a blue sky with fluffy white clouds. The brothers still in the sky were currently behaving themselves. He coughed and felt water rising from his lungs and rolled on to his side and coughed it up. With a sandy hand he wiped his mouth and carefully sat up. Looking around he couldn't believe he was alive but he had no idea where he was or how long he had been carried.

He felt weary to the bone and bruised all over. He wanted a bed and a bath to wash the salt crusted on his skin and a shave. He also needed a piss. His stomach grumbled and he remembered he hadn't eaten nor drunk anything for at least three days and then for however long his Dragon Lord had carried him.

Before he could find anything to eat he knew he needed to give his God an offering of thanks. He pulled out his knife from its sheath and sliced into the palm of his hand. He winced at the pain as he cut deep into his flesh and the salt was dragged through it with the blade. It had been a while since he had offered blood. He cupped his hand, allowing the blood to pool, as he approached the new calm waters lapping on the shore. He turned his hand and the blood dripped into the sea. He shouted, *"I offer this in thanks as your humble servant."*
The blood was carried away by the sea and he fell to his knees as he pressed his bleeding fist to his chest.

It was another hour before he rose unsteadily to his bare feet. He tucked his knife back into its place and then stretched. He heard bones and muscles protest with pops and cracks. He would do anything for a massage at that moment.

He headed up the beach and spotted steps carved into the cliff face, worn by years of use. At the bottom of the steps was a water eroded cave with a vertical banner outside it with a stylised blue dragon on it. It seemed wherever he was still worshipped dragons in the old ways. Before exploring the cave he leant against the cliff face with one hand as he pissed with a sigh of relief.

The onshore wind was beginning to make him cold and feeling a little guilty he pulled the banner down and wrapped it round his shoulders. He hoped there might be an offering within the shrine that he could eat before venturing up the steps which looked daunting in his current state.

Inside the little shrine was an altar before a stone dragon rising out of cresting waves. A drip from above had covered one side of it in green slime. The bowl that would have held a flame had gone out. Beside it was a dish with a large fish that had begun rotting. Kittal pulled a face at the smell and retreated the two steps back to the entrance.

He sank to the ground and leant against the wall. He would have another doze before making his way up the steps. He felt sure the God the shrine was dedicated to wouldn't object. He hadn't felt this tired for a long time and wondered if he had given too much of himself to the lost God.

Myrskyr shifted restlessly around the room anchored by the chain. Ever since he had seen the scarred man he had felt stronger. He wanted to fight though he didn't know why. He heard a rain shower pass over the city and wanted to be out in it. He kept calling out in his mind for the man to come back. He had questions he wanted answered but there was no response.

He was asleep when he sensed a presence and opened his eyes. A growl rose in his throat as mist swirled around him. Something circled outside of his sight but disappeared, whipping up the mist with a hiss, as a man walked through.

Myrskyr sat up with excitement for before him was the man he wanted. He didn't see that the scar-faced man looked weary and was dressed only in trousers. Myrskyr asked, *"who are you? Can you help me?"*

"You must help yourself till I find you."

"Who are you?" Myrskyr demanded.

"I am Kittal. You do not need to know any more for the moment."

"What did you do to me last time?"

"I tried to heal you. I can not help you at the moment. I gave too much of myself last time and need to build my strength up again. We will meet at some point." Kittal said with eyes half closed. *"I can not stay. Help yourself, you can do it."* He faded away.

"No!" Myrskyr called out, *"come back."* His hands became fists, how dare the man abandon him?!

He felt anger surge through him again and he felt himself beginning to change. He watched as his arms and legs shrank and became scaled and more muscular. His hands and feet became four toed claws. He saw his body stretch and a tail form and curl round to fit the room. His head had changed without him realising. He snorted through large nostrils and he snapped a jaw full of sharp teeth. He forgot all about the other occupant of the room as he pulled the chain from the wall and the ring flew across the small room.

Zhina screamed and rolled off the bedroll as she saw the iron ring fly towards her bed. She lay on the floor in fear. This was different from the last two times. He let out a roar of frustration and it sounded like a thunderstorm in their confined room. She covered her ears and felt sure they had burst from the sound.

With his head down he broke through the back wall of the room and ran out. He pushed up with his claws and began to fly, the chain trailing behind him. He roared again as he circled the palace and then the city in a widening arc. The population cowered in their homes.

He didn't know where he was going, just that he was free. He needed to find the man called Kittal who would be able to answer his questions. He sniffed the air, seeking the man's scent. He caught a hint of it and turned north.

He didn't realise at first but slowly he was sinking

towards the ground. The earth hadn't released its hold on him just yet. Then he began to change. He fell, down through the leafy canopy of trees and on to the ground hitting his head on a root. He moaned, stirred and then allowed the blackness to swallow him.

The couple passed him on their way to market, unsure whether he was asleep or dead. His clothes were torn and there were bleeding scratches all over his body suggesting he had been attacked by bandits. They encouraged their horse to move faster while glancing around nervously, fearing that the bandits might still be in the area. The bearded man reached for his axe and held it tight, ready to defend himself and his wife.

Returning that night they saw the young man still lying under the tree. She pulled her coat closer around her coarse woollen dress as she said softly, "perhaps we should stop. He might be still alive."

"What if it's a trick and we are ambushed?" The husband challenged. He had no desire to stop. He wanted to get home before it got dark.

"We'd have heard at market if anyone was attacked." She pointed out, "if he's alive we can't leave him to be eaten by wolves."

"Fine." He sighed reluctantly and reached for his axe as he climbed down from the cart, "I'll haunt you if I die."

"And what if it's a God testing us?" She asked as she followed her husband down with his help.

"He doesn't look like a God to me."

"Come on." She led the way, stepping over broken branches and twigs. Looking up she remarked, "it looks like he fell through the trees."

The man grabbed his wife and pulled her back, "stop. Look at his skin. He's a demon. Lets go before it wakes up."

Myrskyr's skin had not returned to the colour of human skin. Scales covered his dark purple skin like pox scars. Blood stained his hair and the tree root where he had hit his head.

Aishna pushed pass her husband and crouched down as he said, "he's got to be dead by the colour of him or infectious,

50

come on."

"I don't think so. Look he breathes. He's knocked himself out on the tree root. We can't leave him. If we get him home and get the priest he will know what or who he is." Aishna insisted, "come and help me get him up." She grabbed an arm and glared at her husband.
Reluctantly Daxon approached and took hold of the other arm.

There was a moan from Myrskyr as he was pulled to his feet. He was almost dropped as Daxon fought the urge to run. Myrskyr's feet dragged through the leaf litter and he was heaved into the back of the cart like a sack of charcoal.

Reaching their small farm on the edge of the forest where Daxon produced charcoal and tended to pigs; the couple dragged Myrskyr into their two-room house made of wattle and daub and thatch. The pigs snuffled and rooted around in their woven fenced enclosure under the trees. Further into the trees there was a shout, "go away."

"Gaexon, we're home!" Aishna called out.
Their adult son with black hands from shovelling the newly burnt charcoal marched out of the trees, brushing a few loose hairs off his face leaving a streak of charcoal on his forehead. His brown hair was tied back with a leather strip. He exclaimed, "those damn dragons are at it again."

"I've told you before to create a small one then they'll leave our stack alone." Daxon remarked.
Aishna sighed, "don't worry about that for the moment. Go and get the priest. We need his help."

"What for?" Gaexon asked.

"We found someone on the side of the road."

"I blame you if it's a demon." Daxon announced with a scowl.
"Just go Gaexon."

"Alright." Gaexon unhitched the horse and climbed on to its back.

When the priest arrived dressed in woollen trousers and shirt. His wide sleeved overcoat was green and brown to match the forest dragon temple he watched over. Unlike his court brethren he had boots on. He strode with purpose while trying to contain his excitement. Nothing really happened within his area apart from the local population complaining about forest dragons no one had ever seen. A stranger in the woods was something to talk about.

Daxon and Aishna stood outside their home. Aishna approached first, "thank you for coming."

"Happy to help. What is the problem?"

"Come." Aishna beckoned him into her home, "we found him on the side of the road. Maybe you can identify him."

"I will try." The priest frowned at the man, who looked like his body was one huge new bruise, lying on a straw mattress by the fire with a bandage now round his head. The young man looked more dead than alive.

"He's a demon isn't he?" Daxon demanded from behind the priest.

The priest glanced at the old man, "I do not know. Let me take a closer look. He doesn't look well."

"I think he had a fall." Aishna commented, "he looked like he fell through the trees."

The priest approached the prone young man and knelt beside him, "I have never seen anyone look like this before. It looks like he has scales… I'll have to go look through my books to determine what he is."

"He has a large scar on his back like he was attacked by an animal." Aishna remarked as she crouched and rolled Myrskyr's body for the priest to look.

"That could be from anything." The priest frowned.

"What should we do until we know more?"

"Look after him. We don't know if he is a God or spirit so you'd best take care of him. You won't want him angered."

"What have you done Aishna?" Daxon exclaimed.

"I was not going to leave him on the side of the road." Aishna protested.

"Hmpfh. Well, hurry up and get dinner on the go. I'm going to check on the charcoal, coming Gaexon?"

"Umm… Sure." Gaexon said distractedly as he stared down at the young man. He didn't like the idea of an ill stranger being in his home and bringing avenging spirits down on them if he died.

52

He turned to the priest, "what can we do to protect us?"
   "An offering at the temple." The priest suggested.
   "Some more charcoal for the flame?"
   "That sounds good."
   "I'll bring some later then."

Eight

Hearing the roar followed by a roll of thunder the Empress sat up in bed, alert to her surroundings. Her ladies whimpered on their bedrolls on the floor around her room. She ran to her window, not caring who she stepped on, and couldn't see anything. She pulled the window open wide and ran out into her garden seeking the dragon, finally she had been blessed. Her caged dragons chittered with fear. She called out, "come to me and we can rule together!"

She saw the dark purple dragon circle past and then disappear. In frustration she ordered, "come back." She stamped her foot.

She entered her room as there was a knock on the door. A maid hurried to her with a robe to cover her fine linen nightgown. The Empress accepted the assistance as she called, "enter."

Her steward opened the door, bare foot and hastily dressed. He bowed, "your majesty."

"What is it?" She demanded restlessly. She really wanted to climb her ten-storey high pagoda and seek out the dragon. She had to lure him to stay. She turned to a maid and ordered, "go and fetch General Renner."

"Madam." The maid ran from the room, relieved to be escaping the tense atmosphere which would soon unleash her ruler's fiery temper.

The Empress turned back on her cringing steward with a frown, clearly he had bad news as he shied away from her as if expecting to be hit. She demanded again, "what is it?"

"Myrskyr has been taken." He hadn't believed crying Zhina's

explanation that Myrskyr had turned into a dragon and broken out of their locked room.

"Nooo!" Empress Esperanza fainted. Her ladies went for her as the steward stared in shock. No one had ever seen the Empress do something so feminine as faint from shock. The ladies who had gone for their mistress looked just as surprised.

They all stood nervously around as the Empress was fanned to revive her. She lay on a collection of bedrolls that had been piled up to support her. She turned her head and put a hand to it as she moaned, "Myrskyr, no."

"Your Majesty?" The steward cautiously asked.

"Fetch the girl."

"Yes Your Majesty." The steward bowed and hurried the room, taking a deep breath of relief that he had escaped the highly perfumed room that hid the smells of old age and unwashed bodies.

Zhina did not want to go before the Empress. She had never been in front of her. When the Empress had come to the chapel she was expected to remain hidden while the priest puffed out his chest and carried out the rituals with dramatic flair. Watching from her room she had always wondered if the rituals had always had such silly flourishes; but the Empress liked it.

She resisted as the steward grabbed hold of her arm. He could see that she wasn't going to go out of either fear or stubbornness. He said, "you can't disobey an order."
She still dragged her heels as he pulled her along.

He glanced over her appearance to check she was suitable to be presented to the Empress. He frowned at the linen shift dress she wore which was more suitable for the discreet servants then for someone going before their ruler. He tutted but accepted there was nothing he could do about it especially as he still looked scruffy from having thrown his clothes on.

As they entered the royal bedchamber the Empress looked more like royalty than an old woman. She sat in her chair in a gold robe over an underdress. She had recovered from her foolish weakness and was determined to bury it with her stiff commands. The steward pushed Zhina to the floor "kneel before

55

your ruler."
Shaking Zhina touched the floor with her forehead and didn't move from that position. She waited with growing fear for the Empress to speak.

The Empress stared down her nose at the young woman knelt before her. She had never paid much attention to the girl she had ordered to look after Myrskyr. Now she was all she had to tell her what happened. She commanded, "rise."
Zhina sat back on her heels but kept her face cast downwards.
"Come closer."
Zhina shuffled forward till she was at her Empress' slippered feet.

Empress Esperanza lifted the girl's head with a slippered foot. She looked quite childlike with her petite nose, close eyes and round face with auburn hair starting to grow back. She wondered what Myrskyr saw in the pathetic virgin when he could have been with her. Though no one knew it she had once been what Zhina had been. She had been fully devoted until she had caught the eye of the Crown Prince. To hide her past she had had anyone who was aware of it killed as soon as her husband had come to the throne.

Now she rarely looked in the mirror as otherwise she would just have reality reflected back at her. She knew she was old whenever she looked down at her wrinkled hands but focussed on the many jewelled rings instead. She wanted to pretend that she was still the beautiful young queen and mother, devoted to the Gods as she had promised her mother she would be. "Hmpfh."
Zhina nervously gulped and tried not to look at her ruler. Making everyone jump the Empress exclaimed, "you were meant to look after him, protect him till he was strong again." A whimper escaped Zhina's tightly pressed lips.
"You should be executed for your failure and letting him be taken."
"The dragon is him." Zhina protested and then clapped her hands on her mouth as she realised she had spoken out of turn. She watched in terror for her life as the Empress' eyes widened.

The room all became very nervous and froze in their

positions as the Empress began to laugh and then clap her hands, "finally." She leant forward and eagerly asked, "how did you do it?"

"I didn't do anything." Zhina answered with a frown.

"Did you let him fuck you?" The Empress sneered and then sternly, "you did something, and I want to know now!" She slammed a fist on to the arm of her chair.

"He talked of seeing a man in his dreams." Zhina whispered, "he was eating..."

"What man?" The Empress exclaimed in frustration, "tell me now. Who has been visiting you?" She turned on the chamberlain, "who has been visiting them?"

"No one Majesty." He shook as her eyes narrowed and she studied him.

"Hmpfh." Satisfied he had told her the truth she turned her steely eyes back on Zhina and she demanded, "tell me about this man?"

"He said he came like a dream and had a scar." Zhina carefully said. She knew she needed to give the Empress information but not so much that Myskyr would be easily found.
Everyone kept their eyes averted while also trying to work out how their Empress would react.

She was fighting to hide her budding curiosity. She had never heard of anyone able to enter people's minds or dreams. Not even the best priests in Sunulanda could do that. She remembered the mystic she had sent on his foolish errand and wondered whether there was more to the man he was seeking than she thought. How could she not know of this man? Once she had dealt with the girl she would demand the High Priest collective to attend her so she could interrogate them. With an agitated click of her fingers she called out, "Renner!"
The soldier stepped into view, "your majesty?"

"Send out soldiers, I want him found and brought back to me alive. In fact find this man as well."

"You can't!" Zhina exclaimed before she could stop herself.

"What did you say?!" The Empress demanded, eyes narrowed.

"He's meant to be free. He was never meant to be chained to the wall or locked in a room."

57

"How dare you challenge me. I know what is best for a God." The Empress stood, looming over Zhina who physically shrank, "you are some minor courtier's ill-gotten bastard and nothing more than a servant to the Gods and me. He had every right to do as he pleased to you and no one would have stopped him. Lock her up and make it known she is so. He'll come back for her and then I'll have him and then I'll be unstoppable." She cackled by the end.
Tears ran down Zhina's face as she was led from the room by a guard.

Nine

    Kittal didn't stir when he was found by two men in the shrine; nor when he was put on a stretcher and carried up the steps, round the coast and into a little fishing village. He didn't wake for several days in the house of a fisherman and his wife where he was bathed and put to bed.

    He finally stirred as he heard voices over him arguing. A male voice remarked, "he's got to be some criminal, just look at the scars on him and he defiled the shrine. We should report him to the authorities."

"What if he isn't? He could be a sailor whose lost his ship?" A female voice countered.

"I've not heard of any wrecks."

Kittal moaned, "please..."

The two stopped and looked down in surprise.

Kittal winced and squinted in the light of the lamp being held over the bed and croaked, "please… too bright."

"He's awake." The woman, white hair in a long plait over her shoulder smiled down at him, "welcome back to the living. We weren't sure whether you were ever going to wake up."

The man moved the lantern away, letting Kittal's eyes focus.

    Kittal tried to sit up and as he became more aware of how his body was feeling he realised his hand had been stitched and bandaged. The woman held him up and put a hay stuffed pillow behind him. She smiled kindly, "now we can get some broth into you."

"How did I get here?" Kittal tried to clear his throat and licked his dry lips.

59

"My husband and the priest found you."

"You defiled our shrine by sleeping in it." The man said sharply.

"I did not mean to offend."

"See!" The woman exclaimed triumphantly.

"Where am I?"

"In Tapaizu." The woman answered.

"Which is where?"

"Sunulanda." The woman frowned, clearly the man in the bed was not from Sunulanda.

Kittal's eyes widened briefly as he now knew which country he was in and it was the right one.

"Nerysi, we should let the priest know he is awake as we need to decide what to do with him." The man remarked across the bed, ignoring that Kittal was in the bed and awake, and feeling triumphant that the man was a stranger to Sunulanda.

"Later." Nerysi answered sternly.

The man walked from the room grumbling.

"Don't mind him." Nerysi smiled at Kittal, "so, I am Nerysi and you are?"

"Kittal. Thank you for stitching my hand."

"How did you do that?" She asked with concern.

"An offering to the Gods."

"Are you a priest from where you are?"

"You could say that." He carefully said.

"Now, rest and I'll be back later with some food."

"I would be grateful for a drink."

"I will get you something." She smiled at him.

He closed his eyes. He wondered how Lulizen was doing and realised he was missing her. This was one of those moments when he was wishing he wasn't the ruler of Keytel with all the added responsibilities. As a normal family man he would have been thinking about passing on his duties to Tania and Canaan but that wasn't to be. He would have to wait till Ozanus was old enough. If he had been home they would all be around him with Lulizen fretting and the children bouncing on the bed or running round the bedroom.

Then he began wondering if he would ever see any of

them again. How could Ozanus rule Keytel and the dragons without him to guide him? There was no one else to guide him, not even Ciara. What would Lulizen do? He began to imagine her like Tania, life slowly draining from her. And Tania... He wished he could help her but not even the Gods' powers within him could stop her miscarrying. He had changed fate drastically once and didn't think he could get away with it again.

What would the Gods do if he didn't find their missing brethren? He didn't even want to think about that. They could haunt him and drive him mad. They could torture his mind and body in hundreds of different ways. They could destroy his family, leaving him all alone. They could turn the dragons he cared for against him. He knew they were capable of anything when seeking revenge.

He woke up, breathing heavily and rapidly as if waking from a nightmare. He realised he needed to meditate and refocus and calm his mind but he couldn't do it while lying in a stranger's bed. He swung his legs out from under the blankets and tried to stand but they gave way under him.

Downstairs Nerysi heard the thump on the floorboards. Both she and the priest glanced up at the ceiling where dust fell. Her husband had gone to the tavern. To the priest she said, "I'm taking him something to eat, would you like to talk to him?"

"Yes, then I have to notify the authorities. We can't have strangers defiling our shrines and wandering around unrecorded."

They found Kittal pulling himself up. He looked across as they entered. Nerysi gave the priest the tray of food as she tutted at Kittal, "you are not well enough to be up."

"I need to meditate." Kittal said as she put an arm around him and got him back on to the bed.

"Nerysi says you are a priest from wherever you come from?" The priest, dressed in a green coat with white edging imitating waves over a woollen jumper and tunic with trousers tucked into boots, asked suspiciously. He had never heard of meditating being part of worshipping the Gods.

Kittal eyed the young man. He had no idea whether his name or titles carried any weight in this country. They believed in the

61

Dragon Gods and worshipped them in the old ways that Keytel had stopped doing some ago.

He wondered whether there were any dragons even to be found in Sunulanda for dragons used to be captured and used as sacrifices, as well as man, to their own Gods to ensure good weather, harvests and wealth but a side effect to that was a more violent world and raging Gods. For Keytel they'd realised long ago that to care and work with the Gods was better for all and their world became more peaceful, on the most part as man still caused violent stirrings.

He decided to go carefully and not reveal himself so as not to arouse suspicion or questions on why he was in the country. If he could get away from the village he could make his own way to Bakamon and maybe find the missing God before anything bad happened; if not this 'pet' sounded like a good starting place. If it wasn't the right man, he would decide what to do next once there. Stiffly Kittal answered the man's question with a white lie, "I am. Do you have somewhere I can meditate?"

"You should give an offering in thanks that the Gods didn't let you drown." The priest remarked sternly. He was still full of enthusiasm for his role and had yet to be run down by life in the tiny fishing village.

From the edge of the bed Kittal held up his bandaged hand, "I already have."

"A blood offering, very good." The priest approved, "and it seems you are truly dedicated to the Gods." He gestured at Kittal's back.

Kittal pressed his lips together. He had heard of whipping oneself as a sign of devotion from the past but his scars weren't self-inflicted. He had received them while a slave in the mines of Jukirla for a year.

The priest shrugged when Kittal didn't answer, it was personal choice to do such a thing and many didn't discuss why they did it.

"Where are you travelling to?" Nerysi asked as she passed Kittal the bowl of fish stew.

"To Bakamon, your capital." Kittal looked at the woman.

"To the temple school?"

"Umm… yes." He lied though he had never heard of such a thing. It did leave him a little curious as it probably had a library which he could explore and gain new insights on the dragons he protected.

"You aren't going anywhere for the moment." Nerysi remarked sternly.

"I think you'd best obey." The priest chuckled, "I'll come for you in the morning and take you back to our little temple."

"Thank you." Kittal said as he dipped the spoon in the bowl, suddenly feeling ravenous.

Further in land, Aishna, Daxon and Gaexon looked up as their priest appeared in their clearing. Aishna asked, "have you any information?"

"Yes and no." The priest answered carefully.
The family glanced at each other with worry. Aishna said, "go on?"

"I think you have our Empress' missing God." The priest said as he glanced towards their house.

"What do you mean?"

"Do you remember the story of a man falling into Her Majesty's audience chamber during a storm?"
Aishna and Daxon glanced at each other and then back at the priest, "go on."

"She was convinced he was a God and then a few days ago he vanished from the palace. He fits the description I have just received. She has sent the army out to find him and take him back to Bakamon."

"How did he get here then?"
The priest shrugged. He decided not to reveal one crucial piece of information, that the young man had flown away from Bakamon as a dragon. He also needed to decide which side he was on, did he let the army know where the God was and reap the rewards and watch the family die? Or did he keep quiet and hope they never reached this part of the forest? Then he could use the dragon to benefit his own desires. He didn't want to be stuck in the miserable forest temple forever. He was sure he was made for bigger things.

63

"What do we do?" Daxon asked.

"I will support you in whatever you decide. Only the four of us know he is here." He threw the decision back at the family, "we have time yet. The soldiers may not even reach here."

"Thank you. We'll talk about it." Aishna said with a bow of her head.

She turned to her husband once the priest had left. She could see he was struggling with a thought she didn't like the idea of. Sternly she said, "no we are not."

"If they find out we have him then we will be executed. If we report it before they come we will be rewarded." He protested.

"No." She said sternly again.

"Why don't we talk to him?" Their son suggested, "he must be able to tell us how he got here."

"He hasn't woken yet." Aishna pointed out.

"He is alive though as he talks in his sleep though some of it I don't understand."

"Well, I suppose there is no harm in trying." She shrugged.

"We should take turns watching over him so we don't waste any time when he wakes up."

"And if the soldiers come?" Daxon challenged.

"The priest said he would let us know if they came this way." His son tried to reassure his father.

"Hmpfh." Daxon was wary of the plan his son had just come up with. Already he could feel sharp cold iron at his throat and gulped nervously, "I'm going to look at the charcoal." He stomped off. His wife and son could deal with the stranger. He wanted nothing to do with all of it if he could. He would have preferred to have left the man on the side of the road for the bandits and animals.

Aishna said to her son as she saw him frown, "he'll come round. Give him a bit of space." She put a hand on his arm, "come on, lets see if we can wake him up."

"How? He probably has concussion."

"Show kindness to a stranger and you never know how the Gods may bless you"

"Hmm." He responded, not truly believing her words but followed her into their house if for nothing more than to fetch the peelings for the pigs.

      Gaexon was whittling by the low fire, watching over their guest and keeping an eye on the pottage for his mother, when Myrskyr stirred and opened his eyes. He remained still as Myrskyr carefully sat up with a groan. He watched as the young man's pallor turned from purple to peachy skin pink as he looked round.

      Spotting the young man Myrskyr frowned in confusion, "where am I?"

"On the edge of the Forest of Bown."

"How did I get here?"

Gaexon shrugged, "not really sure though ma thinks you fell through the trees. You were looking pretty bad for a while, all grey and purple, like a big bruise, and you hit your head."

Myrskyr reached up and touched the bandage round his head.

"Who is Kittal?" Gaexon asked.

"What?"

"Though you were unconscious you were talking." Gaexon said over the wood he was whittling to a point absent-mindedly.

"I'm not sure."

"You kept calling out for him and asking to know who you were. Do you know who you are?"

"I was given the name Myrskyr." Myrskyr admitted, "I don't remember any of my life before the Empress took me in."

"Why did you leave then?" Gaexon frowned.

"I don't know." Myrskyr looked down at the blanket that covered his legs and picked at a tuft of wool on it, "I just know I wasn't meant to be there."

"She has sent the army out to look for you." Gaexon said sternly.

Myrskyr's eyes widened and his body shrank before Gaexon's eyes. Myrskyr pleaded, "don't send me back."

"Give me one good reason not to." Gaexon remarked stiffly.

      Myrskyr looked everywhere but at Gaexon as he tried to come up with a good reason. He was saved by Aishna entering with a basket of wild garlic to add to the pottage. He turned to see who was entering, getting ready to flee if he needed to.

65

Aishna looked briefly surprised but then smiled, "oh, you are finally awake."

"He is." Gaexon remarked gruffly as he shoved the piece of wood in the fire.

"What's your name my dear?"

"Myrskyr madam. How long have I been asleep?" Myrskyr asked.

"A few days. You must have hit your head hard. Now, would you like something to eat? I'm afraid it's not much as we haven't slaughtered a pig yet."

Myrskyr felt a craving for a large raw bloody piece of meat but that didn't stop him wolfing down several bowls of wild garlic flavoured pottage. It seemed turning into a dragon had left him extremely hungry. He mopped up the juices with a crust of bread.

Aishna watched with a motherly smile as Myrskyr ate. After the conversation with the village priest she had lots of questions she wanted to ask. As Myrskyr sighed, now satisfied, and pushed the bowl away, she couldn't stop herself, "are you really a God?"

He looked up, suddenly wary, "what if I am?"

She held up her hands in peace, "I mean you no harm."

"I am not going back." He snarled and her eyes widened with fear as she saw his fist become a dragon's claw as he slammed it on the table. The air in the room grew dense and throbbed briefly.

Gaexon was up in an instant, having seen the claw as well, grabbing a stick from the woodpile. He demanded, "what are you?"

Myrskyr was staring at his hand which wasn't a claw anymore. He felt Gaexon standing over him and cowered, "I don't know."

"Perhaps we should let the soldiers know you are here. You clearly aren't a man."

"No!" Myrskyr flew up off the bench sending Gaexon flying backwards. He felt himself changing and tried to calm himself. He needed these people to help him. He didn't want to go back to the palace. He had to find this Kittal who seemed to have the answers. He spun round and ran out of the door leaving Aishna and Gaexon staring in shock.

Mother and son stayed where they were, frozen to the spot, not believing what they had seen. After a couple of minutes they slowly released their breaths and looked at each other. Aishna whispered, "we don't tell anyone, not even your father." Gaexon nodded in agreement as he stood up. Carefully he asked, "what do we do?"

"He clearly has no idea he is a God."

"Maybe this Kittal person can help, but who is he? Do we ask the priest?"

"No. The priest will just get suspicious and have more questions." She said sternly, "you'd best go find him and reassure him."

Gaexon nodded again and threw the stick back on the woodpile before heading out.

He found Myrskyr huddled behind a tree at the edge of their clearing. Trying to sound bright he said, "I never got to introduce myself."

Myrskyr looked up, "I'm sorry."

"I'm Gaexon. Come and help me with the charcoal."

Myrskyr saw that Gaexon had come empty handed and slowly stood and followed.

As they walked together down the well-trodden path through the trees Gaexon said, "we aren't going to tell anyone."

"Thank you."

"But you need to help us as well. You really scared us. I want the truth. Are you a God?"

"I don't know. I don't remember. I only started turning into a dragon a week ago when a man came to me in my dreams and then he came again a few days ago." Myrskyr confessed and then with urgency he added, "I have to find him."

"Is he this Kittal you were calling out for? Here, grab that shovel and we'll get the turfs off." Gaexon pointed at the tools they always kept by their charcoal pits.

"Yes." Myrskyr answered as he did what was ordered.

"Perhaps we can help you find him if you can tell me more about him. Do you know who he is? Do you know where he lives?"

67

Myrskyr shook his head and then remembered, "he has a scar on his cheek." He paused and looked at Gaexon, "does that help at all?"

"Not really."

"Oh." Myrskyr was disappointed.

"At least you are free to find him rather than stuck in the palace." Gaexon pointed out.

"And I'll pay all of you back somehow."

"Come on, this charcoal won't come out by itself."

"Yes, of course." Eagerly Myrskyr began helping though he didn't really know what he was doing. It was exciting to feel free and have no walls keeping him in. He felt he could happily live like this forever if the family would let him stay. Maybe this was all he needed. He grinned at Gaexon as he shoved the wooden shovel into the soil covering the charcoal.

Ten

The priest ran into the clearing but the ten mounted soldiers weren't far behind. He cried out as he tripped on the edge of his robe, "they are coming."
The horses swerved round the fallen man, their riders dressed in breastplates and leather jackets and armed with hooked spears and swords. Aishna turned to Myrskyr and shouted, "run! Run!" He froze to the spot.

"What is going on?" Daxon demanded.

"We are looking for the Empress' God and..." The leader of the group spotted Myrskyr from atop his horse and sneered, "I believe we have found him. You are under arrest for the kidnapping of a God."
The rest of the mounted soldiers moved forward to circle the family.

"We did no such thing." Daxon exclaimed.

"I beg to differ since he is standing behind you."

"I'm not going back." Myrskyr protested, glaring at the captain, "leave them alone."

"Get him." The Captain shouted. Then sneered, "her majesty is missing you terribly."

A soldier swung off his horse and made to grab Myrskyr. He didn't get far as with a roar of anger and joy Myrskyr morphed into a dark purple dragon. His blood ran hot, as if this was what he was born to do, to fight. The sound wave generated by the thunder roar sent the soldiers flying from their horses. The family and priest cowered with hands over their now bleeding ears. The horses reared up with neighs of distress and turned tail and galloped off. One was too slow and it got snapped at by Myrskyr. Its head and neck went down in one swallow.

The soldiers stumbled to their feet and gazed up at the dragon that was now curled defensively around the family, filling the clearing. They had all scoffed over their ruler's silly belief that the man was a God, but now before them was the truth. The tail whipped out, taking their feet from under them.

Scrambling to their feet they turned and followed their horses. The dragon uncurled itself and chased after the soldiers, trees were pushed out of the way as he brushed past them. They had no chance of escaping. With several snaps they were all dead and swallowed. The dragon roared again, thunder echoing round the clearing, and turned with a smirk on its face. The expression slipped as it saw the terrified family and then slowly he began to shrink into Myrskyr who dropped to his knees breathing heavily.

Slowly the family stood up, their ears ringing. They stared at Myrskyr, not sure whether to be afraid or in awe of the God that was before them. Daxon made the decision. He dropped back to the ground and kowtowed to their immortal guest, "please do not hurt us O Noble Lord. I hope you are happy with the care we have given you."
His wife and son quickly kowtowed as well but looked up from lowered heads to see how Myrskyr was reacting.

There was silence. No one moved as Myrskyr stared at his hands, he felt a strong desire to keep fighting but men were too easy. He wiped his mouth with the back of one and smeared blood across his cheeks and hand. His eyes were drawn to the body of the horse. He could smell the warm blood and wanted more.

He turned as the priest shuffled across the dirt. The priest said, "O Noble Lord, come with me and I'll take good care of you."
Already he was thinking of the money he could make from charging visitors to see the God. And then there was the esteem; before he knew it he would be out of this dump and maybe even the Empress' personal priest. He was already at an advantage as he had seen her pet turn into a dragon.

"Don't Myrskyr." Gaexon said as he cautiously sat up, "you'll be a prisoner again."

70

Over the last few days the two young men had done a lot of talking and he knew all about Myrskyr's life in the palace. He also knew that Myrskyr had liked a maid just by the wistful tone when he had spoken of Zhina.

Myrskyr looked at Gaexon and then at the priest. He stood and approached the priest who shrank as he sensed the malicious power within the god. He gulped before suggesting, "think of the worshippers who will come and give you offerings."
Myrskyr stood so close that the older man had to look up. He was taken by surprise as Myrskyr grabbed his fat neck by a claw and lifted him into the air. With his free hand he drew a sharp curved claw down the priest's front, cutting through his clothes. The priest wet himself as he struggled to breath. His eyes bulged in his red face as the claw cut into flesh and bone. Blood poured out, staining his clothes. He watched as the god's claw went into his chest and pulled out his beating heart. Myrskyr smiled and licked his lips as he said in the language of the dragons, *"mmm, the corrupt heart of a man and this one will be particularly tasty I feel."*
He stuffed it into his mouth as he dropped the priest's fat body. His eyes rolled into the back of his head as he enjoyed the taste of the blood. He turned to the family, *"for the kindness you have given me I will not eat you."*
They weren't sure whether to be worried or relieved as they didn't know what he had said. With mixed emotions written on their faces they watched as he strode into the forest with all the assurance of an immortal. Aishna asked of the others, "shouldn't we go after him? He doesn't know the forest."

"No. We don't want to anger him." Her husband answered sternly.

It was several hours before the sense of power and invincibility wore off and then he returned to thinking himself a human with all of its confusing emotions and thoughts. He was aware he was finding himself but still didn't know who he truly was. One thing for certain was he wasn't going to let neither man nor beast use him. He needed to find Kittal and in a brief

71

moment of frustration he shouted, "where are you Kittal? Who are you?"

He looked around and realised dusk had descended and it was growing dark and chilly. While there was enough light he quickly made up a fire as Gaexon had taught him.

Sat by this small fire in his torn clothes he began to wonder whether it had been a wise thing to head into the woods. It had been a different person who had walked away from the family. He wondered how Kittal was considering the last time he had spoken he had said he'd given too much of himself. Was helping him turn into a dragon going to eventually kill the man? But it felt good to be a dragon; it felt right, better than the human skin. He liked and was also afraid of the feeling of power it gave him.

He looked around for a weapon when he heard rustling at the edge of the circle of firelight. Dark shapes moved and then stopped. Red eyes blinked at him from the edge and then three small dragons slunk into the light with mottled scales of green and brown. They chattered and chirped at Myrskyr and at each other as steam drifted from their nostrils.

More came out of the shadows, heads bobbing as if they were excited by what they saw. As he tried to work out whether the pygmy forest dragons were friend or foe he realised he could understand them. He demanded, "how do you know I'm a God?" A dragon stepped forward from the group, their leader, a scar blinding one eye, *"they have been seeking you."*

"Who have?"

"Your noble brethren. The first they knew you were alive was when she-who-lives-in-the-moon spotted you before you were hidden again. You are a God and need to return to the heavens. You are needed up there to balance your brothers."

"I am meant to find someone called Kittal who said he would help me. He is an old man with a scar on his cheek." He put a hand to his left cheek, indicating where.

The forest dragons turned and confided with each other before turning back to Myrskyr, *"you mean the Nejus? The High Priest to all dragons, the Lord Defender of us."*

Myrskyr looked mystified. Whoever he was these earthbound

dragons clearly held the man in high esteem.

"I don't know. How do you know of him?"

"He was the prophecy. He was given the powers of the High Priest by the Dragon Lord himself so he could free the dragons on an island. One came past this way when they were freed. He lives in a valley where all dragons are safe to live as they wish. He will be able to help you find out who you are and return you to the heavens."

"He must be the man who came to me in my dreams. Where does he live?" He eagerly asked.

"Across the seas."

"Oh." He hadn't expected that answer. How was he meant to travel across the sea?

As if it had read his mind the leader of the group said, *"you must go back to the family who make the hot black wood piles. They will be able to help you."*

"You think?"

They all bobbed their heads and chirped in agreement.

"I don't think I can get back there. I think I'm lost."

"We'll show you the way when the sun begins to rise." The group's leader said as the others chattered to each other.

"Thank you. I'd best get some sleep. Why do you like the charcoal fires?" Myrskyr asked as he yawned and curled round the fire as if he knew the sparks from it wouldn't harm him. A select few of the group cautiously approached the fire and scratched at the embers before turning on the spot and then curling up.

"We like the heat." The leader answered. Though they puffed steam none of them could breath fire like their giant relatives. It didn't stop them being drawn to any heat they could find. The charcoal pyres were good for their quick hatching eggs if they could dig into one before they were chased off.

With a head butt Myrskyr was woken as the dawn glowed orange through the trees. The group of dragons had shrunk to a select group who were to lead Myrskyr back to Daxon's clearing. They jumped up and down excitedly. Their scarred leader asked, *"are you ready?"*

73

"Yes."

"My children will take you back to the hot black wood piles." He eyed the five sternly and they stopped bouncing and lowered their heads submissively.

"Thank you."

"I am not coming but I hope to hear you again soon."

"Hear me?"

"You are the Thunder Dragon." The scarred pygmy dragon revealed.

"Do I have a name?"

"Not that I know of."

"Thank you for telling me that."

"The Nejus will be able to tell you more. Now, off you go."

The five pygmy dragons called out excitedly, *"this way."* They climbed a tree with curved feet designed to grip the curved edge of tree trunks and branches. They jumped from branch to branch and from tree to tree. They spread their wings so that they soared across any larger gaps that a jump wouldn't be enough for.

Myrskyr had to jog to keep up with them as they jumped and sung. They sung their song of reverence to the Gods which had no words.

Before he knew it he could see the dismantled charcoal kiln through the trees. The dragons stopped. They looked down at him from the branches of a tree. They called out, *"good luck."*

"Do you know they make the small one for you to use so you don't disturb the big one?" He remarked, thinking it was one way he could thank the forest dragons.

They looked at each other and then at Myrskyr again. One asked, *"do you mean it?"*

"Yes. Use it and I'll let Daxon and Gaexon know that you won't disturb the big one anymore."

"Thank you, thank you."

"Just don't over run the forest." Myrskyr warned with a smile, the God briefly revealing itself.

"One life is always lost to a cluster of eggs." One of the pygmies solemnly said.

"Thank you again." He waved up at the dragons before

74

walking away.

He surprised Gaexon as he entered the main clearing. The man was feeding the pigs but stopped at the sight of Myrskyr. He dropped the bucket in his surprise and the pigs squealed with delight and crowded round the spilt acorns. Gaexon exclaimed, "you're back."

"I'm sorry about yesterday."

"It was incredible and terrifying. I never thought I would be standing before a God." It was probably going to be the most exciting thing to happen in his life.

"I need your help." Myrskyr asked solemnly, "I need to cross the sea."

"Why?" Gaexon frowned.

"That is where the man who can help me is."

"All right. Well, we'll have to go to Harvan and see if we can get on board a ship."

"We?"

"Well, you are going to need help getting there and finding passage. Also I think you'll need someone to help you control your temper so you don't turn into a dragon. You don't want to be caught and taken back to the Empress do you?" Gaexon's face had lit up with the excitement at the thought of an adventure. Myrskyr looked thoughtful, "you are right. When can we go?" He didn't want to delay any longer now he knew where he needed to go.

"Let me tell my parents, pack some things and get you in some new clothes and then we can go." Gaexon grinned.
Myrskyr grinned as well.

Eleven

Kittal winced as he tried to meditate again. For the last few days he had been trying to recentre himself but he was finding it harder than`` usual. This time it felt like his heart was being squeezed of all its life. He was starting to think he had been foolish to try and heal the God from such a vast distance as now he could sense when the man started to turn into a dragon, draining him again. He didn't even have the energy to connect mentally with the God to tell it to be careful.

Knelt on his knees on a thin cushion he stared across the small wooden temple. The wood shingled roof was low over the half open wooden walls. The shutters were pulled back to let the spring sunlight in. At one end of the rectangular building was the altar with the stone bowl holding the flame that wasn't allow to go out. Behind it was a wooden statue of the Dragon Lord rising out of faded painted flames.

Though he didn't feel strong enough he needed to keep moving. His garden of tranquillity had ominous dark clouds over it though the children still playing and Lulizen still smiled. With a sigh he rose. The young priest who had been discreetly sitting outside slipped in, "did it go well?" He could sense something powerful in the older man and could see it by the way he walked though currently there was a weariness to the steps as well as if weighed down by too many responsibilities.
Kittal shook his head, not in the mood to share his secrets.

As they stood on the porch a man ran down the village's main and only road. Reaching the temple between breaths he shouted, "soldiers are coming!"
Kittal turned to the priest with a frown and the priest shook his

76

head in reply, "not me."

Yes, he had thought about it, but something had made him consider it would be a foolish idea. However, there were others who appreciated a good reward from any number of groups including the priesthood. He added, "go now, I'll try and delay them."

"Thank you." Kittal grabbed the man's arm as he added, "you won't be forgotten."

The man who had alerted them stared as Kittal's arm glowed and it flowed into the young priest. Neither of the two men involved seemed to notice.

Kittal turned to leave from the front.

"No, through the back."

With a nod Kittal hurried back through the temple and out through a narrow slit of a door.

Staying behind the houses he made it back to fisherman Podraig's four room cottage. Podraig looked up from where he was mending a net while Nerysi scrubbed at a pot. Standing before them, hand on the dragon headed handle of his knife, he said with urgency "I'm sorry, I have to leave now."

"Oh?" Nerysi stopped washing her pot and looked at their guest.

"I would like to give you something for looking after me." He got out his pouch and pulled out a couple of coins. He pressed the coins into her raw hands, "I am grateful for everything you have done for me. Thank you."

"Be careful out there." Nerysi said with concern as she closed her hands round the coins. Later she would realise they were from Keytel and she wondered whether their guest hadn't been not just any traveller. "The forest is full of wild animals and wild men."

"I will be fine." He reassured her.

"I hope you find whatever you are looking for." She gave him a hug while clutching tight to the silver coins, "let me get you some food for the journey."

"No, there's no time. I've got to go but thank you."

Outside the village he had to jump into a ditch and crouch down low as the soldiers and another rider passed by.

At the temple five soldiers on horseback had come into view shortly after Kittal had left, wearing the badge of the Bakamon priesthood, home to all the best priests. The village priest was surprised word had travelled so quickly of their village's guest. The horses' heads jerked back as their riders pulled hard on their reins. Leading them was a priest in a pressed and clearly new long riding jacket over a linen shirt that had been bleached and long riding boots. He looked down his long nose at the young priest who was holding himself taut in an attempt to not shake. The young man stumbled on his words, "can I help?"

"We are looking for two men, one old and one young. The old one has a scar on his face. They maybe travelling together or separately." The priests wanted the man before the Empress got hold of him. The man had intrigued the Head Priest and he wanted to try and convince the man to stay in Sunulanda and use him somehow. Did the man even know what he was?

"What sort of scar?" The priest asked to hide any reaction to the question.

The priest on horseback glared at his inferior for such a foolish question and demanded, "have any strangers come through here recently? I have heard there might have been one who arrived by sea."

"Here?"

"Yes, here. By the Gods, how did you pass your exams?!" The older snapped and the horse side-stepped nervously in reaction. To the men behind him he ordered, "take him."

Two of the soldiers got down off their horses and advanced on the priest. They grabbed the man but leapt back as if their hands had been burnt. They looked at their gloved hands and the leather was singed. They stared at the priest who looked just as shocked.

With a scowl they advanced again and this time they were flung away without even touching the young priest. The priest, up on his horse, narrowed his eyes.

The young priest's back straightened as he sensed the power inside himself. He stared straight into the other's face and

said, "you may as well leave. There has been no one here of your vague description."
The elder was still a moment as their eyes locked. Finally he reacted, "hmpfh. Don't think this will be forgotten." He shouted to the soldiers, "we move on!"
The horses whinnied as they were kicked into movement and continued on down the road. They didn't see Kittal hidden in his ditch as they weren't looking.

As for the young priest he released his breath and sank on to the porch of the temple. He stared at his hands as the villager exclaimed, "wow! Did you see what you did?! You've been blessed."

"You saw nothing." The young man looked up and said sternly,

"Yes sir." The villager shook at the stare he was receiving and then fled.

It took the rest of the day for Kittal to reach the edge of the forest. Following the road he passed fields being prepared for sowing. Others had cows and sheep in. It reminded him that soon it would be the Blood Moon Festival when the moon glowed red and it was time to give offerings to ensure a good crop and large healthy families.

Once there use to be dragon and human sacrifices to the Gods for those blessings but that didn't happen any more in Keytel. Now it was a ceremony led by the women who represented the embodiment of fertility especially when pregnant. There were even rites that even he didn't know about and which were passed down from mother to daughter. He began wondering what Lulizen would offer this year. In previous years she had offered some of her own milk or a blood-stained cloth when she had had her monthly bleeding.

He passed quietly, unnoticed through a town and several villages once he had smeared mud on his face to hide his scar. Dressed in a well washed and patched shirt, trousers and coat he looked like any other farm worker or tramp and no one gave him a second glance. He saw no other soldiers.

With the evening he created a pile of sticks and

murmured a spell to light the fire. He leant against the tree and closed his eyes having already chewed his way through the bread crust Nerysi had pressed into his hand. He had a two day walk through the forest ahead of him followed by another day to Bakamon. With some physical exercise he hoped he would sleep deeply.

Setting up camp the following night he stepped away from the road and into the forest to deter any potential thieves. He had seen a few travellers on the road, including a troupe of mounted soldiers but they weren't the same ones who had come through the village. There were brief exchanges of what was ahead and he brought food off those who had some to spare. Many sensed something different about him and then within the hour had forgotten they had even spoken to him.
As he ate the piece of meat pie he had brought by the light of the fire he heard leaves rustling. He paused in his eating and cocked his head. He called out, "reveal yourself."
There was chirping and then he saw glowing red eyes at the edge of the circle of light and on the trees. As he focused on them he realised he was surrounded by pygmy dragons. He had heard of them but hadn't expected to see them since none were to be found in Keytel. Considering the way the people Sunulanda worshipped the dragons in the old way he was amazed they hadn't all been captured.
News had spread fast through the forest dragon population that there was a God walking the earth and he was going across the sea to find the Nejus. Never had they thought they would see their Lord Defender in person. He had been spotted the previous night but they had been unsure at the time. Now they knew it was him. They chattered excitedly and then their leader, one who had lost the tip of its tail, stepped towards the fire.
Kittal watched in amazement as the leader boldly stepped into the light. He cautiously said, *"hello?"*
The leader bowed its head before chatting and chirping.
Kittal frowned. They were clearly trying to communicate but he couldn't understand them. Their language seemed more primitive

and older than the one he could speak. He said, *"I'm sorry but I don't understand."*

He watched with curiosity as a few of the dragons sidled towards the fire. He asked, *"do you like the heat? I can make a bigger fire?"*
They seemed to understand him even if he couldn't understand them as they all looked at him and nodded eagerly. He smiled, *"all right, let me get some more wood."*

With the wood gathered and the fire spread out for them all the dragons snuffled and settled in the embers, contented, steam rising from their nostrils. Never had so many been accommodated as they curled up in the glowing embers and flames. Kittal watched over them with a love for all dragons, big and small. The few lying in the original fire laid an egg each. Come morning they would have hatched and the dragons who had protected the egg would have turned to ash.

They had all disappeared back into the trees when Kittal woke in the morning. He saw the broken shells and wished he had been awake to see them hatch, to see the pygmy dragon's life-cycle happening. He spread the ash before heading back to the road.

Twelve

Fields merged into houses and shops which then abutted the original walls of the enclosed city. Banners and bunting were being hung in readiness for the Blood Moon Festival. Stalls were being set up for the week long festival. Guards stood at the double gates which were wide open. A queue of drenched people, from a brief heavy downpour, waited to go in via a smaller door while others headed out, flowing around horses and carts like water round rocks in a river.

Inside the walls the buildings were squeezed in with some extending up to five storeys tall. The streets were narrow apart from the main road leading up to another walled city with a tall pagoda covered in scaffolding at the centre of it. Its bronze walls reflected the sunlight, dazzling anyone who looked up at it. Within those same walls, which were topped with the same red tiles as the pagoda's curved roofs, was the palace and temple complex with gardens.

Kittal joined the queue waiting to go in while listening to the conversations going on around him. Most were of the mundane everyday sort while others were on the coming festival, "do you know who is to be the sacrifice this year?"
The companion shrugged, "no idea. Lets hope it's better than last year's. We could do with a better harvest."

"There's been no battles this year so no good captives." The guard, within hearing, input, "maybe a dragon should be sacrificed but they are hard to find."

"Isn't half the army out looking for two men?" The first, a

bearded man from one of the outlying villages asked.

"Yeah and just my luck I'm stuck on guard duty in the rain." The guard, dressed in a helmet topped with a dragon and chain mail over a padded tunic, holding a spear, remarked as it started raining again.

Along the line hoods when up, hats lowered and heads shrank into collars to deter raindrops from dripping down backs.

"Have they been found yet? They've wrecked my house, turned over all my furniture." Someone else asked, "I don't want it happening again."

"Nothing yet." The guard answered as from within the walls of the gatehouse came the shout, "next!"

The queue shuffled forward and there was a sigh as the next in line found shelter from the rain under the stonework.

When it came to Kittal's turn he found a pox scarred man wrapped in a fur edged robe and a large soft cap with a feather in it. An ink-stained right hand from writing names in a big book before him held the pen at the ready. The gatekeeper looked down his nose at the man before him and Kittal decided he obviously dressed to make himself feel more important than he actually was. The man sniffed as if he could smell something bad. He held out his clean hand, "papers."

Kittal frowned, "I don't have any."

"No one is allowed in the city without papers." The gatekeeper glared, "guard get rid of this foolish provincial."

"No." Kittal protested. He held out a hand at the guard who found himself unable to move his feet. He tried to lift a foot and exclaimed, "what have you done to me?" He lowered his spear and aimed it at Kittal.

Kittal glanced at both men and then at the queue who was peering down the line to find out what the commotion was. Behind him those leaving stopped to see what was going to happen. He wanted no trouble but feared it might happen. Looking at the gatekeeper he declared, "I am Nejus of Keytel and seek an audience with your queen."

He released the guard and the man stumbled forward. Hopefully he had done enough to demonstrate he was not to be messed with.

83

The gatekeeper snorted in derision, "ha, and I'm her lover. Never heard of you."

"She will have."

The gatekeeper looked Kittal up and down. He certainly didn't look like a man with a title since he was dressed in the clothes of a poor man and dirty from his travels and in need of a shave. And word would have come from Harvan if he had arrived in the port town. He decided that Kittal was a lunatic who needed to be locked up for the safety of the city. With an inky finger he pointed at Kittal, "guards, arrest him! He is a danger to the city."

Kittal instinctively gripped his large curved knife. He didn't understand what he had done to antagonise the man and now the situation was beginning to spiral out of control as more guards appeared. Everyone stepped out of the way, but continued to watch, as the other guards from either side of the gatehouse came round. They ran towards Kittal who pulled his knife out and growled a warning. They paused, spears aimed at Kittal.

"He has a knife, stop him!" The gatekeeper shrilled from the safety of his kiosk. The guards stepped closer, imprisoning Kittal in a circle of points.

He wasn't inclined to go easily. He'd already wasted a week trying to get well enough to travel to Bakamon and then the four days getting here.

They were prepared for him to charge at them so was taken by surprise as he ducked down and slashed at one of them with his knife. The soldier staggered backwards in shock, staring at the blood pouring from cuts that had gone deep into the bone. Kittal turned on bended knee and threw his knife at another and it sliced the young man's face. While the knife was in the air he turned and grabbed the wildly waving spear and pulled it from the man's hand. He twisted it so that the shaft hit the next one in the circle. With the downward arc of the swing he tripped a fourth one up who landed heavily on his back with a grunt of dispelled air. The last two retreated with their colleague weeping blood and tears as he clutched his face.

The audience retreated even further as the gatekeeper leapt up, red faced, as he screamed, "stop him! I'll give anyone a gold coin who can stop this lunatic."

The incentive of gold was enough to draw a few strong armed men out of the crowd. Kittal eyed them warily as he retrieved his knife one handed and wiped the blood off on his trouser leg and put it away. He held the spear tucked loosely under his arm as if it was a staff rather than a spear, the spearhead pointed towards the ground behind him.

"What are you waiting for?! He's only one man!" The gatekeeper screeched.

The men glanced at each other and then charged at Kittal. Kittal, though breathing heavily, was ready for them. He swung the spear like a pro, knocking the men out or tripping them up. He didn't want to harm any of them. They were foolish men tempted by money.

Then there was another stand-off. The crowds shifted uncomfortably, wary. The official may want the stranger arrested and he was clearly a danger but no one wanted to try and catch him. No one wanted to get near that spear or knife and end up either injured or dead.

Kittal allowed his breath to calm. He wanted to leave and try another day or find another way in but wasn't sure how the crowd would react if he dared move. He slowly stood from his fighting stance but still kept a firm grip of the spear. He knew he would not last another bout. He took a step towards the edge of the circle and the audience moved around him like a swirling eddy.

They turned as there was the sound of shod hooves on the paved road. Leading a troop of cavalry dragging a line of chained men behind them was a tall bearded man wearing a helmet with a dragon as its crest. The crowds parted to let them through silently staring at the dishevelled prisoners. The captain of the group, as he reached the nervously shifting circle, demanded, "what is going on here?"

He looked down at the blood on the ground and the groaning men. The gatekeeper looked relieved. With a pointing finger he exclaimed, "he's mad and doesn't have any papers. I'm trying to arrest him for the safety of our city but he is resisting."

"But he is an old man." The captain sneered.

Kittal glared at the man and retorted, "not so old that I can't take

on you and your men."
He didn't let anyone call him old. Only he was allow to know it through his aching limbs and muscles.

"We'll see. Men, arrest him and he can join the rest of the prisoners."

The crowd gave the horsemen room to dismount. With swords in hand they advanced on Kittal.

Kittal closed his eyes and tried to find the energy within to give himself strength. With reluctance he opened his eyes. He dropped the spear and reached for his knife, the weapon he was more comfortable with. He calmly and sternly said, "I do not wish to kill you, any of you. I have come for your Empress' God."

"She will not release him willingly." The captain remarked with a laugh, having not heard that the Empress' pet had escaped, "and certainly not to a man like you. Stop delaying and get him!" The first horseman swung his sword to knock the man down but Kittal stopped the swing with one hand as he slashed at him with his knife. A gasp rose from the crowd as they hadn't expected such strength. The horseman retreated; his pride bruised along with a cut in his belly.

One of the men who had been knocked down staggered to his feet and wanted revenge for being made to look foolish in front of his friends. He fisted his hands together and hit Kittal on the back of the neck. Kittal dropped like a stone, knife falling from his hand. Everyone breathed a sigh of relief and those at the back began to slip away, the excitement over. A few without papers like Kittal slipped into the city while everyone's attention was distracted.

Thirteen

She had had breakfast and lunch, listened to her councillors waffling on and then sent them all away so she could what she did best, nothing. A musician was quietly strumming a harp in one corner of her room. The windows were open though it rained outside and a cool wind blew through making her attendants shiver. Empress Esperanza didn't notice as she was wrapped up in several blankets next to one of two fires in the room. She declared, "I'm bored. Ouch, not so hard." She glared at the maid rubbing cream on her feet.

Her attendants all froze, afraid that she would pick on them to entertain her. None of them enjoyed doing it as they had all learnt that there would be punishments if she wasn't amused. Currently there were no new attendants wanting to please. The steward at the door gulped nervously, waiting for his Empress to demand where Myrskyr was.

She had seen a selection of men who matched her description the night before but as none of the army had ever seen Myrskyr they had grabbed anyone who looked like a possibility. She had raged but was now calm. At least she had seen that they were obeying her orders. Thankfully she had been asking for him less and less. The Blood Moon Festival was occupying her mind as no special sacrifice had been found, yet.

The Empress looked round at her attendants and pointed at a maid who accidentally caught her eye, "you. Tell me, is there any scandalous gossip? What's happening in the city?" The steward resisted interjecting that she should leave the palace more often. The maid hesitated and looked to anyone who might

87

rescue her. No one made eye contact. She looked back at her mistress who was staring at her intensely. The Empress demanded, "well?"

"Well…. There was an incident at the main gate."
The Empress frowned and looked to the steward. "what is this?"

"It was nothing madam, just someone claiming they are the Nejus of Keytel, whoever that is."
The Empress sat up, now attentive, "Nejus?"

"Yes."

"Did he come with his dragon and his riders?" She eagerly asked.

"Err… No madam. He's just a mad man. He was dressed like a commoner."

"Then how did he know the title?" She pointed out before ordering, "bring him to me."
With a sigh the steward bowed his head, "yes Your Majesty." She smiled with the excitement. He could only hope she didn't get too angry when she was disappointed.

Kittal came round on a cold hard floor. He hoped that when he opened his eyes he would actually be lying on the cracked paving of his valley's ruined temple looking up at the millions of stars like he had done when he was a boy. Back then he had marvelled over how many dragons had died to create them all.

It wasn't to be. He opened his eyes to a damp cell with a floor covered with a sparse layer of mouldy straw. He groaned as he carefully sat up and rubbed his aching neck. His groan was replied to by several other moans. He looked round the room by the light of a tiny barred window near the ceiling and saw several men sleeping in heaps of straw. A bucket was sat in one corner in a puddle. He asked the men and hoped to get an answer, "where am I?"

"In jail." Was a grumbled reply.

Everyone sat up and looked to the door when there was the sound of footsteps. A gruff voice declared, "the newbie doesn't get anything until he's proven himself worthy."

"Yeah." Three voices chorused.

88

Kittal just stared at the door. He needed to get out. He really didn't want to find himself a prisoner again. His hand went for his knife but he found its sheath empty. Nothing was going right and he silently swore at the Gods for getting him involved in their mess.

The door swung outwards revealing a guard and the Empress' steward. The guard pointed his hooked spear into the room as he growled, "keep back."

"Where's our food?" The leader of the group of prisoners demanded.

"Coming soon if you behave."

"That the man?" The steward pointed at Kittal who slowly stood.

"Yes. Caused trouble yesterday at the gates." The guard remarked before shouting, You!" The guard gestured at Kittal with his spear, "you're coming with us. Now, no trouble or you'll find yourself back here."

Kittal said nothing as he obeyed. Now was not the time to cause trouble.

Once out of the jail, Kittal, hands tied behind his back was marched between two guards with the steward ahead of them. He asked, "where are we going?"

"To the palace."

Kittal didn't react as at least now he was heading to the right place.

He was led through the palace complex via the back entrance. They came through the stable yard where horses were being brushed down and then into the servants' corridors hidden in the walls before stepping into the main corridor, empty of courtiers as ordered by the Empress. She wanted no one to see her visitor and be seen as a fool if it really was just a madman.

He was brought before the Empress who sat on her throne surrounded by her ladies. She was dressed in gold brocade with strings of pearls and her dyed hair was piled with hair ornaments. She wanted this man to be in awe of her if he was just a commoner otherwise she wanted to impart the power she had. She fought revealing her emotions as she was eager to see if this really was the Nejus travelling in disguise and if he

89

was, why was he here?

The Empress grimaced at the sight of the man before her, why hadn't her foolish steward had him cleaned up first? He had clearly not shaven for a few days and his clothes were covered with she didn't want to know what, and he smelt. She did have to admit there was a proud bearing about him and he wasn't in awe of her. He stood before her tall and alive with power, but she could see no scar. This was definitely a man whose appearance hid his true being. She fought a giggle of excitement.

She sat straight, thrusting out her aged chest to try and look more impressive. She demanded, "who are you to claim to be the respected sovereign of another land?"

"That's because I am." Kittal answered sternly with a straight face.

"If you really are the Nejus of Keytel where are your dragons?"

"Safely at home." Kittal responded stiffly and suspiciously. It was potentially a good thing he hadn't arrived on the back of Kite considering Sunulanda still worshipped the dragon gods in the old ways.

"Hmm. Prove it."

"I shouldn't need to."

She glared at him as he wasn't giving anything away. Until he was cleaned and properly dressed she couldn't definitely be sure.

She beckoned one of her oldest companions forward and softly said, "take him to a suite of rooms. Get him cleaned up and dressed but make sure there are guards. I will watch from the servants' passage."

"Madam." The woman curtseyed. She didn't show any reaction to her orders as she was used to her ruler's strange requests. She stepped down from the dais and crossed to Kittal, "please, come with me." She carried on past him.

He looked to the Empress who said with a smile that didn't reach her eyes making him wary, "please, rest, eat and we will meet again later."

He curtly nodded his head and then followed the Empress' woman from the room.

As he left he thought the Empress was certainly an intriguing woman. He had made no real first impression of her. Perhaps later when they re-met he would be able to get to know her for he realised he knew little about her. She was far across a sea so not a threat to his lands, yet; so he had had little reason to understand her and her lands.

Once in a suite of rooms he was glad to remove his borrowed clothes and sink into a tin bath of hot water beside the fire. He lay low in it with his knees sticking above the water. He only rose out of the water as a barber was ushered in to shave him and trim his hair.

From behind the wall, in the servants' passage the Empress watched through one of the many peepholes used by servants and lecherous courtiers alike. She watched him rise from the bath, water dripping from scars and taut muscles that were clearly still being used unlike her useless husband's flabby ones. He pulled on a robe held out for him and then sat in a chair to be tended to by the barber. She thought him handsome for his age and she felt she might swoon with a growing desire she thought had dried up a long time ago. She wondered if he would be interested in her.

She knew it was the Nejus of Keytel once the stubble had been removed and he turned his head and she saw the scar on his left cheek pulling the corner of his mouth up. For anyone in the know knew that was his distinguishing mark caused by his grandfather's dragon as a child.

Was this the dream walker the girl had mentioned? If so this could be bad for her if he found HER God. He wouldn't relinquish him if he did find the God.

She found herself giggling at the fact she had the man as it meant her God would come looking for him. She covered her mouth so he didn't hear her. She turned to her companion who stood a discreet distance away, "get a feast prepared for our esteemed guest."

She continued to watch as another two servants entered with food and clothes. She couldn't quite hear the words but by the tensing of muscles she guessed he didn't like the choice of

91

clothes and felt disappointed. Laid out on the bed was the clothes of a priest of the richest luxurious fabrics, how could he not want to wear them considering one of his several titles was High Priest?

She watched as he reluctantly put on the fine linen shirt, loose breeches and wide sleeved gold cloth robe. It felt heavy on his shoulders and not just because of the weight of the fabric. He had a feeling there would soon be expectations thrust upon him especially as the Blood Moon Festival was coming.

He didn't want to spend any more time than necessary in Sunulanda. He wanted to find the God and then leave with him and get home to the safety and familiarity of Keytel and his Valley home. Once there he could go about getting the God back to the heavens.

He came up with an idea of a plan as he ate the cold meat, cheese and bread brought for him and drank the wine which was too rich and spicy for his tastes. He would go for a wander once everyone was asleep if he could work out how to get into the passageways hidden in the wall and see if he could find the God. Hopefully if he had a good night's sleep he would then be able to open a portal and then he could get the God away from the Empress. He'd only done one once before and that had transported himself and Lulizen from her mountain palace home to Keytel. He rarely used the skill.

Fourteen

He would have preferred to have just slept and working on centring himself to rebuild his energy, but he found himself attending a feast as guest of honour. He was escorted to the Dining Hall where trestles covered with cloths and benches had been set up for the court.

At such short notice the kitchens hoped that with enough alcohol the courtiers wouldn't realise the offerings were on the poor side. There were spit roast chickens and ducks and bowls of pickled vegetables raided from the stores as well as some salted beef. Cabbage was slow cooked with spices and plenty of bread was baked to soak up the sauces.

The Empress appeared oblivious. She felt like the shy young girl she had once been, glancing at Kittal beside her through her eyelashes. He could feel her looking at him and chose to ignore the attempts at flirtation. He had no interest in her whatsoever. She turned to him and smiled sweetly at him, "so, Nejus, what brings you here?"

"I heard an interesting story of a man falling through the roof of your home." Kittal carefully said. He didn't know what she knew about the man.

"Oh." She responded with false disappointment. "I thought perhaps you were here for something more important than some silly man who fell through my roof during a storm. It was certainly a surprise to have you arrive dressed as a tramp. You should have a sent a messenger and I could have organised a better reception." She would have the cooks whipped later for the poor array of foods for a feast

"I didn't plan to arrive like so but the ship I was on sank." He lied as he reached for an apple.

"Why did you not come on your dragon? Do you know we worship the same Gods? You are just in time to help us celebrate the Blood Moon festival."

"It was too far for Kite to fly and I am aware of how you worship. We have moved away from the blood sacrifices and the keeping of dragons chained up."

"But the Gods require it, demand it." She exclaimed, "how can you have their blessings if you do not?"

"Because I look after them. I honour and protect the dragons in exchange for the Gods' blessings." He frowned. He looked at her and felt some relief that she was a three week journey away from Jukirla and Keytel. The thought of her corrupt belief in herself and the gods in his valley scared him.

"But think of the power we could have between you and me and with your dragons." She proposed.

"No thank you." He said stiffly and stood, "it has been a long day so please excuse me." He didn't want or need a treaty with the woman who had several sides to her of which he had seen only two of them so far. She was also evading his first question making him think there was something amiss.

The court stared at Kittal and then at their Empress as he crossed the Hall. Everyone became tense, waiting to see how she would react as no one had ever defied her. They watched her stand and shout, "I have not given you permission to leave." Kittal stopped and slowly turned. He glared down the hall at her. She shrank before his gaze. He didn't need to do or say anything for the strength of the powers bestowed on him by the Gods radiated out from him. He remarked slowly and carefully so everyone could hear, "I do not need your permission, or anyone else's to leave this room. You think yourself blessed by the Gods, well I actually am. I carry the blood of the original High Priests within my veins and the powers bestowed upon them." He turned and walked out of the door. With a wave of his hand the doors slammed shut in the faces of the two guards who were

94

about to escort him through the palace.

Everyone stared, stunned by what had just happened. The Empress quickly sat back down, her pride bruised. She shouted, "continue…. Now!"

She stared at a point on the floor a few feet in front of the dais, scowling, as the conversations slowly returned and rose in volume and the musicians began playing again. She was not going to let Kittal get away with this. No one undermined her. And she was not going to let him anywhere near her God wherever he maybe. How could a dragon hide so well? Why had no one seen it?

Kittal sat cross legged on the bed trying to calm himself. The Empress was definitely one to watch. There was a silent deadliness to her. He wondered when the palace would become quiet enough for him to sneak around. He had seen servants come through disguised doors in the panelled corridors and wondered how many secret passages there were.

An hour later he felt it was time to make things happen himself. He needed to pass through the palace and temple unseen to find the missing God. He couldn't make himself invisible but perhaps he could make everyone sleep or at least turn a blind eye as he slipped through the corridors of the palace and temple.

He left his room via the window in his shirt and breeches with a brief glance at the door. While on the windowsill, toes clinging to the edge of it, he reached up to haul himself on to the roof. Staying low he headed up the wet tiles to the ridge and paused surveying the landscape of buildings below him.

The palace was set up with the ruling family's quarters at its centre where the audience chamber and Dining Hall were also to be found. Behind it was the Empress' garden enclosed by a wall.

Surrounding the large rectangular building and garden was a one storey building and a two storey building. Within the two outer buildings which acted like a wall around the Empress' rooms were the rooms and offices of the courtiers plus the palace's chapel to the Dragon Gods and rooms for guests. Against the wall enclosing the palace and a large courtyard were

95

the barracks of the palace guard, stables and kennels and storerooms.

Opposite the palace across a paved dirt yard with a raised stone path was the temple and its library and school for priests. Like his ruined one in the valley it was made of stone arches carved with dragons holding up a roof that covered the front half of the building that held a fire that was kept continuously alight. The rear half was open to the sky so the gods could see the sacrifices given on the altar. At the top of the steps, in front of the temple, was another altar for public display with a large roughly hewn stone. Dried blood stained the top and sides of it and also pooled on the step around it.

Perched on the ridge in the drizzle Kittal could only hope what he was about to do would work. He pressed his hands together, fingers pointed up and took a few slow deep breaths before he drew his hands apart, the power of the Gods expanding between his palms just like it had done at Jurikla six years previous. He began to raise his arms as he continued to part his hands, the power growing to surround him and the buildings. He twisted his wrists so his palms faced downwards and slowly brought his hands down. The invisible energy field descended on the buildings and inside everyone sagged where they stood, sat or lay, eyes drooping and becoming blind to their surroundings.

Kittal sagged himself where he was straddled across the ridge, his head resting on his chest. With a deep breath and sigh he lifted his head, now it was time to explore in peace. He carefully moved back down the roof as the tiles were slippery and dropped on to the roof of the lower building and then jumped down into the yard from the edge of the roof. He first headed to the Empress' garden where he could sense dragons. He walked along the path which was lined with cages. Several were empty but then he heard chattering from one. He paused, *"hello?"*
A few pygmy stone dragons, with mottled bumpy skin as they tended to live in stone walls or cliff faces, crept out of the shadows of a pile of rocks, *"help us."*
  "Why are you here?"
  "We were captured for her pleasure."
96

"Are there any others?"

"Look." The leader of the little group gestured with its head. Kittal turned and now saw the glow of a skinny shrunken fire dragon, scales crusting like lava cooling in the air, and surrounding it a group of forest dragons using its internal heat to stay warm. He asked, trying to keep the disgust and shock out of his voice, *"is this it?"*

"There was the sense of a God but that has gone." The fire dragon lifted its head and murmured.

"I was sent to find the God." Kittal remarked, *"but first I will free you."*

"We tried to get his attention when he came into the garden but he always looked lost as if he had forgotten who he was. Then by chance She-who-lives-in-the-moon saw him and he began to change but not quickly enough as the clouds hid her." The fire dragon remarked as if he hadn't heard Kittal.

"Who is he?"

"The Thunder God. You should have heard him when he was freed."

"And where is he now?"

"Don't know. He flew away." The dragon said apologetically. Kittal swore to himself, all that energy spent getting to Bakamon wasted.

"He always had a girl lingering around him," The dragon commented thoughtfully, *"she may know where he has gone. Find her."*

"Thank you. Now, let me free you all."

"Just let me die." The fire dragon said mournfully, *"I am too weak to fly anywhere. I was always too weak which is why I was captured."*

With a click of his fingers the cage doors unlocked. With a nudge of a snout the pygmy stone dragons opened their cage and slipped out.

Kittal opened the cage of the fire dragon and crouched down beside it, *"I'm sorry this has happened to you. I'm sorry I couldn't have protected you."* He placed a hand on the dragon's snout, *"but it is an honour to give you peace."*

"It is an honour to have seen our protector on earth himself.

97

We had only ever heard of you from those that passed through. "
    "Sssh, now rest. " Kittal softly said.
The dragon began to smoke as its belly grew brighter, going from red to yellow to white and then flames began to dance on its scales and they in turn grew bigger until its whole body was ablaze. The forest dragons chirped in excitement and got so close that they were soon alight as well. Kittal stepped back and watched as the dragons' bodies rapidly burnt to nothing.

    His anger radiated from him and the sound of breaking bars grew louder as the cages broke one by one before collapsing on themselves so they could never be used again. Now, though, he had to see if he could find out if the God had truly gone and where it might now be.

Fifteen

Ever since Myrskyr had escaped Zhina had been locked in a store room with a rotating selection of grumpy guards. She knew the Empress was waiting for Myrskyr to come back and rescue her but didn't think that was going to happen. She knew enough about the Gods to know they weren't that interested in the men and women of the world unless they could do something for them. Now Myrskyr was free he wouldn't be coming back, not even for her. He would be seeking out this Kittal person.

But that person seemed to have arrived in the city according to the two guards outside her storeroom cell. She sat on her straw mattress tucked in the corner of the room listening to some snuffling mice in the bags of grain and to the guards.

She became alert as the guard's voice drifted off as if he was falling asleep. She heard a clunk as if the lock in the door had been turned. She cautiously slid to the edge of the mattress, wrapping the blanket tighter around herself. She lingered, afraid of what might come through the door. Nothing happened. She stood and approached the door. She put a hand to the door and pulled it open. She peered out and was surprised to find her guard still standing but slumped against his spear. She waved her hand in front of his face. His drooping eyelids didn't even blink. She looked round in confusion, what had just happened?

She quickly decided not to hang around. Though it was cold on her feet she padded across the yard and to the palace. She had to find either Myrskyr, Kittal or both, though she didn't know what the second looked like.

As she made her way through the palace she found more guards, servants and courtiers slumped wherever they had been caught by whatever spell they were under. She began to wonder why she had been spared.

She certainly didn't expect to find anyone else. She spotted him ahead of her, walking with purpose around a corner. As the only other person awake she ran after him hoping he might have answers to her questions.

Rounding the corner she found he had disappeared. She frowned as she paused and then realised ahead of her was the room she had been locked in with Myrskyr. She slowly approached and peered round the door frame. The hole made by Myrskyr had been blocked up temporarily with wooden planks. The man she had spotted stood in the middle of the room.

He turned and both of them looked surprised at the sight of the other. She didn't recognise him and was a little frightened by the scar pulling his mouth into a sneer. She stammered, "who are you?"

His eyes narrowed and he muttered, "is it failing already?"

"Everyone seems to be under some sort of spell but you aren't?"

"That's because I did it. The Gods seem to have decided that you aren't to sleep."

"Who are you?" She demanded.

He looked her over and she felt naked under his gaze. He saw a young woman in a dirty shift wrapped in a blanket with auburn stubble for hair. Her face was thin but looked like it was better suited to being plumper like Lulizen's. He finally answered her question, "Kittal."

Her eyes widened, "are you who Myrskyr is looking for?"

"Myrskyr?" He frowned, "I don't know who that is but I am looking for someone."

"Yes. Myrskyr is who you want." She responded eagerly, "he didn't know your name."

"I'm looking for someone who fell out of the sky."

"That was Myrskyr."

"Where is he then?" Kittal demanded in frustration.

She took a step backwards, afraid of him. She didn't know whether he wanted to harm Myrskyr or not. Cautiously she asked, "what do you want from him?"

100

"You don't need to know." He answered stiffly, "now, tell me where he is. I know you know."

"No." She responded stubbornly, "how do I know you don't want to harm him?"

He sighed. He was not in the mood for arguments and defiance. He was tired and the girl before him was delaying his search and his eventual retreat to bed. He snapped, "if you are not going to help me then get out of my way."

"No." She defied him.

He glared at her, "I don't want to hurt you but I will...." He let the warning sink in and saw her gulp nervously. She stepped out of his way and watched him walk down the corridor.

She wondered if the only chance to help Myrskyr, wherever he was, was slipping out of her hands. Did she risk it? It wasn't like she knew where he was, just that he had escaped the palace. She made a decision and ran down the corridor as she called out, "wait, please!"

Kittal stopped and turned. With a scowl he said, "I hope you aren't going to waste my time?"

"Umm.... No...." She stammered, "you aren't here to harm Myrskyr are you?"

He decided on the gentle approach, "I'm here to help him."

"He turned into a dragon." She cautiously answered.

"I know."

"You do?" She was surprised.

"Where is he....?"

"Zhina." She answered.

"Please, the spell is not going to last forever and I don't want to be found here." He commented sternly.

"He turned into a dragon and broke through the wall and flew off but I don't know where to." She finally revealed.

Kittal rolled his eyes and sighed in frustration, this mission had just got harder. To Zhina he said, "thank you." He nodded his head and began to walk away. It was time to think and sleep.

"Wait."

He paused and glanced back, "what?"

"Do you know what he looks like? I can come with you. I have nothing here. I've been locked up as the Empress thinks he will

101

come back for me."

"Ha. Gods are selfish beings. He won't be coming back."

"I know, but..." She wasn't sure whether she dared reveal her attraction towards Myrskyr.

"Come on. Lets get back to my room and we will talk there." He said as he looked round, sensing something amiss. The spell was degrading. With urgency he added, "hurry up, we don't have long before they all come round." He began to run out of the central building and back to his own room. Zhina briefly hesitated before following, he would potentially be let off if found but she wouldn't.

She shut the door behind her as Kittal got the fire going again. He pulled off his damp clothes, oblivious to Zhina's presence, and put on the bed robe before sitting on the floor by the fire warming his hands and bare feet. He remarked, without looking at her, "don't stand by the door. Get rid of that blanket and wrap yourself in that gold robe. Then bring that jug of wine and cups over." He put the poker into the heart of the fire to warm. He'd rather not have wine but there was nothing else.

She moved cautiously across the room, side stepping round the edge so she could keep her eyes on him but he didn't seem interested in her at all. She let the blanket fall and grabbed the priest's robe. It swallowed her in its folds and dragged across the floor as she crossed to the table with the jug and cups. She rolled the wide sleeves up before she carried the tray to the fireplace and sat opposite Kittal.

He stuck the hot poker into the wine which hissed and produced a puff of steam. After pouring them each a cupful he sipped at his as he studied Zhina. She shifted uncomfortably under his gaze again.

"So what are you to him?" He asked sternly.

"Nothing I guess from what you said earlier." She said, feeling her eyes watering, "I thought we were friends." She stared into the cup of wine.

"Hmm..." More softly he asked, "who are you?"

"Zhina. I used to be the maiden that tended the flame in the palace chapel and then I was nursemaid to Myrskyr as Her Majesty finally realised that he wasn't eating and growing

102

thinner and thinner and now I am nothing, just bait it seems."
She ended bitterly, "he's not coming back is he?" She looked
across to Kittal.
He shook his head, "I don't think so but you are right about one
thing. I don't know what he looks like in human form, only as a
dragon. I'm going to need your help."
"You mean it?" She asked hopefully.
He nodded, "I'll get you some clothes and then we'll get out of
here as soon as we can. I'll probably have to stay for the Blood
Moon festival. Now," he finished his wine and stood, trying not
to groan from aching limbs, "it's time to sleep."
She glanced towards the bed; did he now expect more from her?
She gulped nervously as he shrugged off his robe revealing a
back covered in scars. She asked, "where do I sleep?"
"The bed is big enough for both of us. I guess like me you
haven't enjoyed a warm comfortable bed in a while." He turned
and there was a kind smile on his face.
"You won't touch me?" She asked with fear as she stared at his
naked body and tried not to look any lower than his chest.
"I have a wife waiting for me at home." He simply stated, "I
just want to sleep. If you don't want to share then you have the
floor." He turned and headed to the bed.
        A warm bed with a feather mattress was too tempting.
She saw he lay with his back to her as she slipped into bed. She
lay on the edge of the bed as far from Kittal as possible who
seemed to have already fallen asleep and wondered how he could
sleep while Myrskyr was alone out in the world. Tears began to
fall as she worried for Myrskyr.

Sixteen

In a mist shrouded world Kittal called out, *"where are you Myrskyr? I come seeking you and find you gone."*
The mist stirred and a dark purple dragon emerged, *"where are you? I head for a land across the seas that you rule."*

"Keytel?" Kittal asked in surprise.

"Yes." The dragon answered with a frown, *"should I not be."*

"No, no." Kittal hastily said, relieved that the god was heading in the right direction and now he needed to as well, *"how are you getting there?"*

"I will fly with a friend. There is no ship going that way at the moment."

"Fly low till you reach an island called Jukirla. You are a God so can get there. Go to Jukir and seek out my daughter and son-by-marriage. They will look after you till I get there hopefully. Find my dragon as well, Kite. She will know you to be a God."

"And my friend?"

"Zhina?"

The dragon frowned, *"no. A man called Gaexon."*

"He will be looked after as well."

"Have you seen Zhina then?"

Kittal saw a glint in the dragon's eyes that didn't show on its face. He was hiding feelings he was confused about. Softly he said, *"she is now safe with me."* He added, *"now you'd best go before your brothers find you."*

"What do they want? What have I done to make them angry?"

"I don't know but I will find out. Go."

The God didn't need any more encouragement to leave. With a

flick of its tail it disappeared back into the mist; just in time as his brothers appeared snarling and growling.

They circled Kittal, snapping their jaws and flicking their tails at him. The iridescent purple dragon crackled with the high energy of lightning. Kittal cried out, *"you do not scare me."*

"Well you should be." The Wind God sneered, it's pearlescence scales growing darker as it grew angrier, *"we can kill you with one bite of our jaws."* A tongue flicked out and rolled over its sharp teeth.

Kittal stood his ground. He didn't feel any fear though they were Gods. He had dealt with too many adolescence dragons to be scared. He knelt down on one knee and bowed his head, *"Lords."*

"Hmpfh." The first sneered.

Kittal looked up and cautiously said, *"your brother..."*

"Do not talk of him. He is not allowed back up here." The Wind God snapped.

"Stay where you are, where you belong human." The Lightning God snapped above Kittal's head.

"You can not help him even with those powers the Dragon Lord has bestowed upon you." The wind dragon sneered.

"I am under the Dragon Lord's orders." Kittal declared and looked the chameleonlike dragon in the eye. He saw a pupil large and inky black but deep within it he saw the other side of the dragon, the one that produced the fluffy white clouds of a summer's day.

The Lightning God swept past Kittal so close the hairs on his arms rose with the static charge. It snarled, *"do not tell him anything brother."*

"You are affecting everything that lives on the land and in the water." Kittal tried to reason, his face still on the dark dragon hoping to bring out the softer side.

The dark dragon blinked first and turned away. With its tail it swept a hole in the mist and Kittal found himself falling.

With a shout he woke up and found himself sat up. He spotted Zhina staring at him clinging to the edge of the blankets while standing as if she had fallen out of bed. Slowly his breath

105

calmed as he said, "sorry."

"You were talking like Myrskyr did in his sleep."

"The language of the dragons." He remarked with a tense smile. He didn't want to frighten her with what had happened in his dreams. For a moment he wished he was back home where Lulizen would have understood and they could have discussed it together. He added, "I know where Myrskyr is."

"You do?" She tried to hide her relief and eagerly asked, "did he ask about me?"
He smiled more kindly, "yes and yes." At the same time he felt sorry for her for a woman and a dragon God would never be able to be together, but nothing was out of the question. The God could prove him wrong. He added, "I need your help to get away from here quickly. The quickest way is a portal but I am not centred enough nor have the mental strength. I need to make an infusion to help. Where would I find someone selling dried herbs, plants and roots."

"An apothecary will be able to help you. I can take you to a good one." She eagerly answered.

They were interrupted as the door opened and a manservant entered and looked confused, "what's going on here?"
Kittal asked quietly, "does he know who you are?"
Zhina shook her head.

"Good." He then turned to the servant, "excellent timing. Find this young woman some clothes and organise a bath for her. She stinks." Kittal ordered with a wink at Zhina who looked confused.

"Umm… Yes sir." The servant bowed. He winced, his head hurt and couldn't explain why and the scene before him was making it worse. It was safer just to obey.

"And some clothes for me as well. I'm not wearing what was given to me yesterday. A shirt and trousers will do me just fine."

"Yes sir." The man retreated from the room.
Zhina giggled.

"I think they are all a little dazed." Kittal remarked with a rueful smile.
She smiled shyly back. Under his stern façade there seemed to be

106

another more friendly person and she liked it. Becoming stern again he added, "now, where were we."

The door crashed open and the Empress stormed in, nightgown and robe flapping around her feet. Her dyed hair was loose down her back and her wrinkles had yet to be hidden by make up. She exclaimed, "how dare you?!"

"How dare I what?" Kittal enquired calmly but sternly as he slipped out of bed, oblivious to his nakedness. The Empress' eyes widened and her mouth dropped open.

"You cast a spell over all of us." A priest declared angrily, stepping from behind his ruler, carefully dressed to impress. He was determined to outshine the visitor claiming to be High Priest of the Dragons from where he came from. His Empress had been foolish to give him the clothes of a priest.

Kittal fought back a laugh as the priest resplendent in gold brocade, which stretched round his fat stomach, and wearing trousers that were cut a little too short revealing fat ankles. A black hat perched like a large fly upon the man's piggy face. He knew of several dragons who would be sorely tempted to eat the man. Kittal felt more dignified standing before them nude then he would be dressed like the priest. Kittal remarked, "because I needed to get answers that no one was giving me." The Empress spotted Zhina, "how did you get out?"

"She's now with me. She gave me the information I needed." Kittal answered for Zhina.

"Traitor. Whore." The Empress hissed and Zhina retreated to press herself against the wall out of fear. The Empress then turned on Kittal, "and as for you. You aren't going to get your hands on my God. He's all mine and mine alone."

"I think it's a bit late for that as he has left the country. Now, if you'll excuse me I must make preparations to leave myself." He reached for the bed robe and pulled it on.

"No!" The Empress exclaimed.

"Madam?" The priest beside her said softly.
She turned on him and angrily demanded, "what?!"
He beckoned her closer as he murmured, "the blood sacrifice perhaps. Imagine what the Gods will bless us with if we offer him up."

An evil smile appeared on her face at the idea and then she laughed, all that power being released she felt sure would bring her God back to her. And with him permanently gone he wouldn't be able to challenge her authority.

Though she didn't realise it the priest was thinking the same thing. Once dead his fellow priests wouldn't get the opportunity to one-up him with new knowledge. He didn't need knowledge to stay one step ahead, just the Empress' patronage. The longer Kittal lived the more likely he was to influence both his queen and the priests he led. He smiled as he watched Empress Esperanza point a finger at Kittal, "as you claim you have been given a gift from the gods I'm sure they would be delighted to have it back. Arrest him. He will be our sacrifice to ensure a fertile growing season and bring my God back to us." Zhina gasped in shock and looked to Kittal to see how he was reacting. He had paled but that was quickly hidden by anger, "I am a guest in your country. Sacrifice me and you'll merely make them angry and blood thirsty. It won't bless your fields."

  "Good, then they will bless my army and I can attack my neighbours for more sacrifices for them." The Empress sneered, "maybe even Keytel and I'll claim my God back at the same time."

Kittal found himself speechless but relieved his country was too far away for her to attack quickly. If she really did get a blessing from the Gods there would be no stopping her. What was worst was after last night he didn't have the strength to stop her right here, in this bedroom. He couldn't even throw the guards off that appeared through the door, one twisting his arm behind his back crippling him while another put his sword to his neck daring him to fight.

Seeing her freedom rapidly disappearing Zhina screamed as she leapt across the bed and jumped on the guard holding the sword to Kittal's throat. The man fell backwards from Zhina's sudden weight on his back, slicing into Kittal's throat as he did. The Empress screamed, "no!"
She feared she was about to lose the best sacrifice she would ever have but he didn't fight to free himself.

Kittal's now free hand went to his throat and found that

though it bled the cut had thankfully not gone deep and
hopefully wouldn't scar either. The guard grabbed hold of Zhina
and threw her to the ground where she knocked her head on the
floor, stunned. A third guard came and pulled Zhina up and held
both of her wrists behind her back.

They were led through the palace and across to the
temple's school where they were thrust into an empty cell along
with clothes and a snarled order of, "make yourselves decent."
Zhina willingly pulled on the skirt and blouse over her shift
while Kittal put on the trousers that were thrown at him. Tucking
the blouse into the skirt revealed her slim body underneath the
shift. She asked, "what do we do now?"
"Nothing." He responded as he shrugged off the robe and
found space by a wall to sit cross legged.
"Nothing?! We are to be sacrificed in four days time." She
exclaimed.
"I am well aware of that." He said sternly as he placed his
hands on his knees and closed his eyes, "now quiet."
A sob escaped her lips and the tears wouldn't stop flowing. She
wondered if the sacrifices in previous years all felt the same and
why didn't they fight unless they had all been drugged. She didn't
like that idea and planned to spit it back in their captor's face.
She cried herself to sleep and woke a couple of hours
later to find Kittal hovering a few inches above the floor. She
stared in astonishment as she hadn't expected that.

109

Seventeen

Over the next four days she silently watched Kittal. Every couple of hours he would awaken from his meditation to piss, eat or drink before returning to his meditating. The power that slowly filled the room wouldn't let her near him. The power pulsed red and gold around his body. Sometimes he levitated but most of the time he sat with his back against the plastered wall of their cell. There were moments when his breathing slowed so much she thought he had died. She wanted to ask what he was doing especially when he smiled, but didn't dare to.

Without the herbal infusion meditation was all he had to build up his strength. He went deeper than he had ever been. Most of the time he sat in a dark space so he could just concentrate his mind, slowing his breathing and his heart before gradually returning it to its normal beat. Then to remind himself what all this was for he retreated to his garden paradise where his three young children played with a radiate Lulizen round with child next to him. And on his other side was Tania looking her normal self, her weight back on, with a baby in her arms, laughing and smiling. It was this scene that kept him strong even if there were dark clouds hovering above them all.

As the fourth day locked in the cell drew to a close the sounds of the school infiltrated his mind. He heard the bell announcing dinner for the novice priests and another an hour later for lights out. He heard footsteps on creaking floorboard as one of the teachers walked the corridor to make sure everyone was in bed.

He was ready.

Outside, in the palace and on the crowded streets, the

Blood Moon festivities began with pipes being played, drums being beaten, and drunken songs sung. Larders had been emptied of everything luxurious which had been saved for this moment and had been consumed by huge gatherings of friends and families. Fireworks lit up the sky in red, greens, purple and white. Dancing happened and young couples slipped away to find dark corners to copulate in. All of it would end with the human sacrifice to the dragon gods and it didn't matter how drunk they were everyone planned to be there as they had all heard it would be an extra special sacrifice this year, the high priest from a far off land no one cared about, along with his recently acquired lover.

Before he could let Zhina know they were leaving the door was unlocked and opened. Armed guards stood outside, wary for they were sure he wouldn't come so easily this time. The steward looked exasperated from having to obey his mistress' latest whim. He pointed at Kittal who had slowly stood, "him."
  "Where am I going?" Kittal demanded suspiciously.
  "The Empress wishes to see you."
Zhina stared in astonishment at Kittal while he showed no emotion.
  The soldiers swarmed in and surrounded Kittal the best they could in the confined space as he pulled on the robe. One pointed his spear at Zhina, aware of how she had attacked one of them earlier in the week. She watched him be led out and then heard the lock turn in the door and once again she was on her own.
  She had felt brave while Kittal had been in the room ever though he had been silent and oblivious of her, but now she let her fears out. Tomorrow she was going to die and not even her parents were going to rescue her. They would think it an honour. Maybe Myrskyr would fly in and rescue her but he seemed to be heading somewhere else that was far from Bakamon and her. She retreated to a corner and hugged her knees as tears rolled down her face. She ignored the food put through the door an hour later.

111

She hadn't been able to get the image of Kittal standing boldly naked before her out of her head. He had exuded a masculinity her husband and son didn't have and for his age he had still looked good even with his scars. She had felt her blood heat up and felt sure she blushed under her make up every time she thought of him and was glad it hid her red cheeks. She wanted no one to discover that her desires had been re-awoken. She wanted to remain the image of cold callousness so no one discovered they could influence her with hotblooded handsome men.

The guards had no idea why she wanted to see the sacrifice and her steward was too afraid of her to put two and two together. None of her women questioned her as she ordered them to make her alluring.

They found one of her finest linen nightgowns with embroidered straps and left the ribbons on the front undone exposing the enticing gap between her reasonably firm breasts which had been lightly dusted with a perfumed powder. Her hair had been re-dyed to a more natural auburn and brushed till it shone. As her best feature most of it hung down her back. Some of it was pulled back into a rough bun held in place with several hair pins headed with dragon heads. Her thinning lips had been painted with dark rouge. She had had her normal make-up scrubbed off and hoped she didn't look too old.

Now she lay in an open gold robe propped up against the pillows and cushions of her bed. She was determined to have a taste of the Nejus of Keytel before he was sacrificed to the Gods. She felt sure he was a man who knew how to give and receive in equal measure. She wanted to feel his strong hands on her, holding her as he thrust into her. She wanted his power and strength to penetrate her and hopefully be gifted some of it.

The door opened and Kittal was pushed in. Seeing he wore the bed robe still and just a pair of trousers she wondered if he knew what she wanted from him. He stood by the door looking stern and as cold as a statue. She tentatively licked her bottom lip as he coldly enquired, "have you realised your mistake?"

112

He gave no indication that he had seen how she was dressed which disappointed her.

"I haven't made any mistakes." She just as coldly replied before ordered, "come here."

"No."

"How dare you disobey me?!" She exclaimed in anger. It was going to turn into a battle of wills and she was determined to win. She sat up, "look at me. Don't you desire me?" Her voice came out plaintive.

"No." He stood his ground. More than ever he wanted to be back home with soft, lithe Lulizen. He felt sure that no one, not even her husband, had desired the Empress for a long time and he didn't plan to be the first.

She slid to the end of the bed and pouted as she stuck her chest out, convinced she was still alluring, "am I not beautiful?" He rolled his eyes and desired several drinks to blot out the image before him. He didn't respond to her question so she slipped off the bed and minced towards him. He thought she would be better off remaining the heartless woman she had personified when they first met.

She stepped up so close to him he could smell the liquorice root she had chewed to hide her bad breath. She grabbed his crotch with claw-like fingers as she hissed, "you are going to fuck me and you are going to enjoy it."

He felt his penis retreat in reaction to her grabbing it and then it betrayed him. He felt it begin to grow and wished he hadn't been thinking of Lulizen. The sex drive he was often proud of was unwittingly reacting to a woman's touch however ugly he perceived her to be. He closed his eyes and tried to calm his blood but it was too late. His body felt breasts pressed against it and he felt his heart beat faster. He was no longer in control of his body as the Empress undid his trousers and began to stroke the hard length of his erection. He decided to mentally shut down and hoped it would then end sooner. He hadn't felt so powerless for a long time. The last time was when he had seen Tania fall from the walls of Titan's castle home.

He allowed the woman to lead him to the bed and push him on to it. As if he had departed his body he watched her pull

113

off her bed robe and nightgown. She sucked on a finger before slipping it between her thighs as she straddled him with her aged body. She rubbed at herself as she grabbed one of his limp arms and pressed the hand of it to her breast. She rubbed herself against his erection then moaned aloud as she came, keeping his hand squeezing her breast.

That wasn't the end of the torture for now she lowered herself on to his swollen erection and began to rock on it with an excited cackle. She threw her head back and dug her fingers into his chest. His body reacted eagerly to her slick warm folds and pulsed as it came a minute later. A shudder went through his physical and mental bodies and his mouth opened with a silent groan.

She moaned with pleasure and disappointment. She had hoped he would have lasted longer. She continued to rock on his rapidly shrinking erection, determined to keep hold of it for just a bit longer. She had forgotten what pleasure could be got from sex and now wanted more.

Reluctantly she got off him. Like a sleep walker he sat up but she pushed him down with a sneering laugh, "I'm not done with you yet."

Kittal retreated further into himself. He could fight her and escape but he didn't think he could get to Zhina as well and he needed her. He had to hope she would eventually fall asleep. He watched as she caught a drip of semen running down the inside of her thigh with a finger and examined it. She looked at him and asked, "do you have magic cum as well? Perhaps you can make me pregnant even though I'm well past it. Just think of the child we could make."

She strolled across the room to where a door had discreetly opened and one of her maids stood, head bowed, holding a bowl of warm water and a cloth. The Empress cleaned herself and then shooed the maid from the room.

With frustration she discovered she couldn't lure another erection out of him, not with her hands, her breasts or her tongue. She had broken her toy and she wanted to beat him but fought the urge. She needed him to be presentable for the sacrifice. She left him lying at the end of the bed and climbed

114

under the covers and slept a sleep that held no guilt for raping a
man, and a fellow ruler. She was glad he would be dying at
noon.

Eighteen

He lay still for a long time until he heard the Empress snoring. He carefully got up and retrieved his trousers feeling ashamed of himself for not fighting harder. He had been in worst situations and fought and survived but he hadn't been able to fight his body's natural urges.

He found a jug of wine with two glasses and commenced to drink the lot to cloud the memory of what he had seen, before falling asleep in the chair he was slumped in. He only woke, groggy and grumpy as the Empress kicked him and ordered, "get up."

As she went to slap him round the face he grabbed her wrist, "enough!"

She shook it off and retreated with a cackle, "prepare to die and no one will be able to save you." Turning to the maids who were silently moving round the room she ordered, "get the guards to take him away."

He could have fought and got away, he was strong enough now. In fact, any time since the Empress fell asleep he could have created a portal and gone but he didn't think it would be right to abandon Zhina to her fate after she had helped him and he might need her still. He let the guards march him across to the temple, across the yard which was beginning to fill with people there to see the finale of the Blood Moon Festival. With this sacrifice lay all their hopes for the year.

Kittal was taken to a room where Zhina already stood naked and wet and red from being scrubbed clean, trying to hide her breasts and pubis. His robe and trousers were pulled from him by two novice priests with rolled up sleeves. He was made

116

to stand over a drain and then water was thrown at him before they scrubbed soap all over him, lathering it up before throwing more chilly water at him to wash it away. He didn't flinch. Then they were both dried with coarse towels.

Zhina was dressed in a red shift dress while Kittal was dressed in a red shirt, breeches and a worn old robe embroidered with dragons which looked more familiar to him then the wide sleeved ones the priests now wore. They wanted him to look like a priest but without ruining any new robes.

Surrounded by novices dressed in grey robes, cinched in with cord belts with strings of beads hanging from them, they were walked out of the school and through the temple. There was going to be no way they were letting their sacrifices escape this close to the event. Zhina reached for Kittal's hand and hoped he didn't feel her shaking. She had spat the drugged drink at the novice who had tried to make her drink it. She wanted her senses clear for whatever Kittal might plan.

They were brought out to the blood-stained altar. Below them the paved yard was crowded with the population of Bakamon. Children sat on their parents' shoulders and daring youths had climbed the palace to perch on the roof to watch. Everyone was more willing than normal this year to be crammed in to watch the sacrifice of the foreign ruler. Their own ruler was nowhere in sight as this was a day for her priests. She would get a report later of any signs good or bad that the Gods had accepted the offering.

Kittal and Zhina were handed over to four albinos dressed in white loincloths with large knives tucked into them. Currently sat on their bald heads were dragon masks. Kittal was impressed that the Empress had managed to find four albinos but as one stepped closer he saw that the albino before him was a fake. He was covered in thick white paint and had brown not red eyes. He lowered his blue crested dragon mask to hide his secret and then grabbed Kittal by the arm. One of his companions, wearing a red horned mask, grabbed the other. The other two grabbed Zhina and held her still.

The High Priest, still too fat for his clothes, strolled out of the temple and smiled at the gathered. In a loud voice, as he

117

held up his hand for silence, he said, "now is the climax of the Blood Moon Festival. This year we have two offerings for the gods so let us pray they accept them and bestow upon us a bountiful crop."

A cheer rose up from the crowd and Kittal was dragged towards the large altar. He dug his heels in and roared, "unhand me now!"

The albinos froze, taken by surprise. The audience wasn't sure how to react, was this part of the sacrifice this year?

Kittal began to glow red and he felt his body begin to heat up. The albinos released their hold of him with yelps of pain and stared at their burnt palms. Looking up it looked like the man was on fire.

Kittal put his hands together to become one large fist and slammed it down on the stone altar as he roared, "enough!"

The stone altar cracked through the centre. The crowd was silent, not sure how to react. The High Priest found his voice, "how dare you?!"

"Silence!" Kittal glared at the man as he leapt on to the cracked altar. He turned to the audience, "this is a festival of fertility. Look to your women and honour them. They are who nurture and birth our heirs. Look to the Gods whose names have passed into history. It is them who ensures there are animals and plants to feed us. These blood sacrifices just needlessly make the gods more blood thirsty."

Conversations began in the crowd and passed back to those who hadn't heard.

He didn't stay to see the outcome. He jumped down from the altar and grabbed hold of Zhina who was surprised to find his hand cold though flames flickered around him. The albinos holding her retreated in fear as Zhina was pulled towards Kittal.

With a gesture a portal shimmered ahead of them though she couldn't see what was through it. She was going to have to trust him as he strode purposely towards the large rectangular portal dragging her with him.

Her eyes widened in surprise as she looked round and saw she was in a dirt yard with a house full of windows and wall on one side and a long wooden building on the other; but this one was empty. She looked to where she had come but found the portal had already vanished and she was looking at two men running across from a barracks. She turned to Kittal for answers and found him on one knee breathing heavily.

One kept running while the other, a young man with a limp and damp brown hair, stopped beside them, exclaiming as he did, "sir!"

"Diego." Kittal responded between breaths.
Diego pulled his Nejus up and slung one of his arms over his young shoulders.

"Has the God arrived yet?"

"Mathieu has gone to fetch Canaan."

"Has the God arrived?" Kittal repeated with urgency.

"I haven't heard anything yet."
Kittal grunted.

"What has been going on? Your throat sir?"

"I'll explain later."

"Nejus!" Canaan called out as he appeared with Mathieu behind him. He didn't even see the woman standing close to him looking bewildered. As he got closer he asked with concern, "are you all right?"

"I will be in a bit. Has the God arrived?"

"Someone called Myrskyr came looking for me saying you sent him. Is that him?"
Kittal looked relieved, "yes that's him." As an afterthought he asked, "how is Tania?"

"She isn't allowed to leave her bed by orders of the midwife."
Canaan answered reluctantly. He didn't want his Nejus to worry while he had a god to deal with.

"Has she been taking that tonic?"
Canaan nodded.

"Good. Do you still remember the ingredients for my tea?"
Kittal asked while still leaning heavily on Diego.

"Yes sir?" Canaan frowned, "why?"

"I could really do with some plus some food and my clothes. Also, Zhina here could do with the same." Kittal glanced at her and Canaan finally saw her, "she's our guest and will be able to
119

confirm that this Myrskyr is who I am looking for.”

“Yes sir.”

“I'll see Tania once I have rested. Don't let her know I'm back yet. I don't want her to worry about me.” Kittal said sternly.

“Yes sir.”

“Come on Diego, help me inside. Come Zhina, Canaan will find you a room.” Kittal looked to Zhina and gave her a tight smile.

Nineteen

Zhina, afraid to be alone in a strange place found her way to Kittal's room once she had been given clean clothes, a pale yellow blouse with a ribbon at the neckline and long skirt, and eaten. She knocked on the door and it swung open as if it hadn't been shut properly by another visitor. She found the room empty but the large window opposite was open and the breeze was stirring the half open curtains.

She found him in a chair on a balcony overlooking the garden. He didn't move and she wondered whether he had fallen asleep but then a hand picked up the glass from the table beside him and he said, "welcome to Jukirla. This island is under my care so you will be safe here."

"Where is Myrskyr?" The fact he was so close made her want to see him and find out what she meant to him.

"Somewhere. We will meet later. I need to rest first." He answered without turning, "have you eaten?"

"I have, thank you." She moved closer and saw he wore a linen tunic with roses and vines embroidered round the stiff collar which hid the red wound on his throat. At his waist was wrapped a red sash.

"How are the clothes?" He didn't move his head.

"Good, thank you."

"Good. Now I'm sorry to do this but can you leave?" He asked stiffly.

"Oh." She hadn't expected that. She saw movement come from the other side of Kittal, "oh, sorry. I didn't realise you had company." She retreated backwards realising that he probably had the job of ruling to catch up on.

121

He turned briefly and she saw that he was weary and the expression on his face was solemn as if he had heard bad news. He gave her a tight smile, "thank you."

She blushed and then ran, feeling foolish that he would have wanted her company still when he was now amongst friends and family. A servant had informed her who were the important people to be aware of as she had helped her get changed. She ran down the corridor and outside and through the garden and out to the barracks where she stumbled to a stop at the sight before her.

Standing three times the size of her was a dark grey dragon, leaning forward on her clawed wings who frowned disappointingly at her. In shock and fear Zhina screamed causing men and women to run out of the barracks calling to each other, "what's going on?!"

A hand covered her mouth and span her round as the owner harshly said, "what do you think you are doing?! Be quiet." Slowly the brown haired man from earlier removed his hand. Zhina's mouth silently opened and closed and she pointed behind her. Finally she whispered, "dragon."

The man laughed at her and called to the others, "false alarm, she's never seen a dragon before."

There were grumbles as they returned to the barracks.

"I'm Diego, one of the Nejus' companions and a Suwar. Do you not have dragons where you come from?"

Carefully she shook her head and asked, "why is no one trying to attack it before it eats us?"

"That is Kite." Diego smiled, "come on, I'll introduce you." He took her by the arm and tried to draw her closer to the dragon. Zhina resisted and Diego said, "suit yourself."

She remained where she was and watched Diego approach the dragon without fear.

"I heard the Nejus is back." Kite remarked with hope. She had missed him and home and wanted him back so they could go home.

"He is." Diego grinned.

"Why has he not come to see me?" She demanded, *"who is that? Even if I wanted to eat her she wouldn't be worth it."*

122

"He is resting. The trip seems to have taken its toll on him."
Diego frowned, *"he would have seen you arrive."*

"Hmpfh." She didn't like Diego's answer.

"Be patient, remember he's not a young man anymore." He carefully remarked.

"Hmpfh." Then just to amuse herself she snapped in the direction of the nervous woman who with a yelp turned and fled. She smirked, enjoying the reaction.

Diego scowled, *"behave yourself."*

"I can do as I please. When he is ready I will be back." She pushed up into the air.

Up on the balcony Kittal saw Kite rise into the air and fly away. He had also seen Zhina running away and frowned. Beside him Tania, wrapped in a blanket, said, "she will soon learn there is nothing to be afraid of."

Her father had already told her most of what had happened to him since insanely jumping off the cliff. She hoped he wouldn't be left with another scar for his collection. And they'd already discussed what he would have to do if Myrskyr was not the man-dragon he sought. He would have to travel back across the seas.

"Hmm..." Her father responded distractedly and then sternly said, "I am glad that my new infusion is working but you should be obeying the midwife."

Tania blushed with the knowledge of her disobedience, "I know but I heard talk you were back and I had to come and check for myself."

"I will have to take the God back to the Valley but I will stay till one way or another." Neither of them mentioned the word 'pregnancy.' They skirted around it for fear that if mentioned Tania would lose it. He took hold of her thin hand and said with pain in every muscle of his face, "and then it must stop. Not just for you but for Canaan as well. You drive him further and further away."

"I don't mean to." She whispered, "I don't like seeing him so far away from me."

"And," he turned in his chair, leant across and cupped her thin face in his hands and felt the tears, "I want my beautiful daughter back, not this pale imitation."

123

She nodded and closed her eyes to hide her father's expression which was making her feel guilty. With her eyes still closed she took hold of his large, calloused hands and held them in hers. As she opened her eyes she took a deep breath and said, "I promise."
He gave her a tight but loving smile, "thank you. I have already sent a Suwar to let Lulizen know that I will be here."
She gave him a tight one back as she silently prayed that the child would remain inside her so at long last she could give her father a grandchild and not feel barren and worthless any more. He kissed her warm forehead before saying, "you'd best go before anyone finds you up."
  "I am glad you are back." She remarked as she carefully stood, hand to her belly as if to cleave the baby within her, to her.

Twenty

Myrskyr had heard that Kittal had arrived on the island and had spent the afternoon impatiently waiting to see him but was never sent for. In the morning he and Gaexon heard that Kittal was down by the barracks and hurried out. Perched on large pots placed against the garden wall they peered over as they saw him return from a flight with Kite. They watched him get greeted by a Suwar and together they went into the barracks.

A while later all of the Suwars came out dressed in their padded flying gear and holding wooden swords. They stood in a circle with Kittal in the centre and Harim to one side with a drum. To a slow beat of the drum they began to attack and defend themselves from Kittal and the two opponents on either side of them. As the drumbeat sped up so did the movements of the Suwars, wooden swords clashing and retreating.

With one last rap of the drum skin the Suwars broke apart sweating, breathing heavily but grinning. They threw the swords in a pile before helping each other out of their padded jackets. With that off they all ducked under the spout of a water pump and received a splash of water before stepping away, shaking water from hair and faces with grins and laughs.

Kittal walked away with a wave of a hand. As he passed by the wall he called up, "I know you are up there. Give me five minutes."
Myrskyr and Gaexon glanced at each other as Gaexon whispered, "how did he know?"
Myrskyr shrugged, "because he is the Nejus?"
  "Whatever that means."
125

"Come on, he said five minutes." Myrskyr said eagerly as it meant soon he might have an explanation for all the gaps in his memory and there was quite a few of them. And then there were his questions, why did everyone think he was a God? Why did he keep turning into a dragon?

True to his word Kittal appeared in the garden five minutes later, dressed in tunic, sash and trousers and his dragon embroidered sleeveless brocade red robe. His hair was still damp from the water pump. Behind him walked Canaan and Zhina. Myrskyr and Gaexon stood nervously at the other end of the path.

Zhina, spotting Myrskyr, gasped and then ran towards him. He looked startled to see her and how she had changed. She looked thin though her hair was growing. Her face was alight with adoration which made him uncomfortable and confused.

Beside him Gaexon saw the running woman and caught her in his arms before she reached his friend. As she struggled in his arms he demanded, "who are you?"

She stopped moving and glared up at the brown haired man and in turn demanded, "who are you?"

"I think some introductions are needed." Kittal remarked with a smile of amusement as he and Canaan approached the three young adults, "Zhina, is this your Myrskyr who turned into a dragon?"

Zhina wiggled out of Gaexon's hold and nodded as Myrskyr looked to Kittal. At the sight of the scarred man from his dreams and exclaimed, "are you the man who came to me in my dreams? Kittal?"

"I am." Kittal stiffly responded, "and you have met my son by marriage and Governor of Jukirla, Canaan. Who is your companion?"

Gaexon stepped forward, "Gaexon sir and you are?" He ended suspiciously.

"The Nejus of Keytel, High Priest of the dragons and High Chieftain of the Suwars so you'd best mind your manners." Canaan answered with warning.

"Now, you can catch up and get to know each other properly later but I would like to speak with Myrskyr alone." Kittal

126

informed them all.

Myrskyr eagerly agreed to the private conversation and stepped through Zhina and Gaexon who were eyeing each other warily.

They left the group behind them as they walked side by side down the path. Kittal paused to pick a pink rose and examine it while trying to decide where to start. Finally he spoke, "what do you remember? Or what have you learnt about yourself?"

"I fell from the sky as a man and that is all I knew till recently." Myrskyr shyly admitted as he watched Kittal study the rose, "I also feel like this is not my true form. Until recently I knew nothing but how to be submissive and obedient..." He tailed off and tried to work out how Kittal was reacting, "now I'm supposedly some sort of God and a dragon."

"That is correct." Kittal looked up from spreading the petals of the rose, "you are one of four brothers. The four of you fought and you were pushed out of the heavens but I haven't found out why yet. You are the God of Thunder."

"You said you tried to heal me. Why didn't I stay as a dragon?"

"I don't have the power to."

"Zhina said I changed under the moon." Myrskyr stated.

"The Moon can be a healing one when the need arises." Kittal responded.

"I change when I am angry."

"It is your nature to. You were born to fight. Without you and your brothers there would be no thunderstorms to cool the heat."

"Why don't I stay as a dragon when I change?"

Kittal looked thoughtful before answering, "perhaps it is because this is not your world. This is the world of man, not dragons that are Gods. Perhaps that is why you remain a man. What I will do is show you meditation techniques that will help you keep your temper under control until we get back to the Valley."

"I like being a dragon." Myrskyr protested.

"I'm sure you do but I can't have a dragon who can't control itself flying around Jukirla. Many of the islanders distrust and are frightened of them still."

"Why can we not go to the Valley now then?" Myrskyr demanded. He liked the idea of being able to become a dragon at

127

will.

"There is much for you to learn as a young man." Kittal chuckled.

Myrskyr scowled, how dare a man laugh at him considering he was a God? He saw one of his hands become a claw. He expected Kittal to look frightened but was surprised that Kittal looked bored. Myrskyr blushed and apologised.

"Thank you. As a God you do not feel emotion but as a man your mind is probably filled with thoughts and emotions you do not understand. Am I right?"

Myrskyr nodded as he realised that the man spoke aloud what he was thinking. He gulped before asking, "will you help me understand?"

"Of course. Now to answer your question. I am a father and I have a daughter who needs my support. Until it is no longer needed we will be staying here. It will give us plenty of time together, teaching you."

"Why is she in bed?" Myrskyr asked carefully, not wishing to offend the man.

"She is pregnant." Kittal answered stiffly. He didn't want to discuss it with the young man beside him. With a lighter tone of voice he went on, "I will find us somewhere suitable to meditate and we'll get together later. For now I think you'd best help Zhina and Gaexon get to know each other. I feel they will help you through all of this. Any questions don't hesitate to ask." He gave the young man a knowing smile.

"Thank you." Myrskyr answered with a frown.

Like a father to his child Kittal gently pushed the young man back towards his friends, "go."

Myrskyr was pleased that Gaexon and Zhina seemed to get on after a few hours of the three of them together. He didn't realise till she sat beside him on the stone bench, swinging her legs, how much he had missed Zhina. She smiled shyly at him when she felt his eyes on her. She thought freedom suited him and was glad he had found someone who wanted to help him as much as she did. Now he knew he was a God she hoped he would start to enjoy what time he had with them and would feel

128

less lost.

Gaexon didn't show it but he was a little suspicious of Zhina. Considering she once had the status of Handmaiden of the Eternal Flame she would probably be wanting it back and not remain an outcast. He felt sure that behind her words she would be scheming how to get Myrskyr back to the Empress and he wasn't going to let that happen. He felt protective of the lost young man. He didn't want his adventure to end either. He didn't want to return to his dirty boring life making charcoal.

They looked up as a shadow of a dragon flew over them and watched it land in the dirt yard by the barracks. Gaexon was in awe of the Suwars already and murmured to himself, "I want to be one of them."

Myrskyr frowned, "what did you say?"

"Nothing." Gaexon blushed.

"How can you not be scared of them? They are huge." Zhina protested, "they could eat you in one mouthful." She shivered in her fear.

Gaexon fought the urge to tell her what he was thinking, go home then and good riddens. He wanted Myrskyr to himself though he couldn't explain why. To distract himself from the thoughts he remarked, "do you think I could learn to fight like them? Like the Suwars?"

Myrskyr answered, "ask and maybe I could too."

"Mmm. I don't think so considering what might happen." Myrskyr scowled in frustration but Gaexon was right. For the moment he wouldn't be able to fight without turning into a dragon.

Diego strode into the garden with his limp, unwrapping his turban as he did. He grinned at the three of them as he said, "I've been sent to fetch you Myrskyr."

"By who?" Gaexon demanded protectively.

Myrskyr put a hand on his friend's arm, "it's all right. It's Kittal isn't it?"

Diego nodded, "the Nejus, yes. Come."

"See you later." Myrskyr said to his friends as he stood.

"Let me know how it goes." Zhina called out as he walked away with Diego.

129

As Diego helped Myrskyr up on to Joli's back the blue tinged dragon bowed its head, *"it's an honour to be carrying a God."*

"Thank you..."

"Joli." The dragon grinned. Long ago now, he had come to realise that being the ride for a Suwar was not a punishment. He loved being it especially with Diego as they had both come to learn they had similar temperaments and easy going attitudes to life.

"Where are we going?" Myrskyr asked as Diego got into his saddle with the help of Joli lifting a forearm.

"Up the mountain. Our Lord has found a place where he can help you." Diego said as Joli lifted into the air.

They were in the air for half an hour before Joli landed on a ledge, slipping slightly on its crumbling edge, high on the mountainside. Snow still lay in patches, protected from the sun by the branches of pine trees. Kite perched above in the sun dozing but ready to go at Kittal's bidding.

Ahead of them Kittal waited in front of a cave entrance in shadow wrapped in a coat against the cold. He remained where he stood as Myrskyr slipped from Joli's back and the dragon and Suwar rose back into the air.

Myrskyr approached, "where are we?"

"An ancient shrine I was told about. Come in, let me show you something." Kittal beckoned the god forward. He led the way into the cave. Though the entrance made it appear dark a diagonal shaft of light lit the back of it up revealing an old altar with a stone carved bowl filled with water which rippled every time a drop of water fell from the moss covered crack in the ceiling. Around the walls were painted dragons of the sea and above them four more in a black cloud. Kittal pointed at the paintings, "this island once worshipped the dragons whose whims affected them most- the sea and the storm dragons of which you are one of four." He glanced at Myrskyr to see whether he understood, "we will meditate here and hopefully the Dragon Lord will speak to us."

"Why did they attack me?"

130

"I don't know. Come, let's sit in the light."

Once settled on the floor, Myrskyr following Kittal's lead, Kittal instructed, "you must find a place of peace within yourself and use that to centre yourself, then whenever you feel yourself getting angry and beginning to change think of that place and stop yourself. Once you can control that part of you then you'll be able to change whenever you want."

"Let's get started then." Myrskyr eagerly said.

"Have you an idea of a place in your mind to go to then?" Kittal asked as he rested his hands on his knees.

"No." Myrskyr frowned, "what is yours?"

"That is private." Kittal smiled as he thought about it, "and so will yours be. It will come to you." Becoming serious again, "now, close your eyes and slowly draw in a deep breath and slowly exhale it. Let your mind go blank." He closed his own eyes and quickly found his breathing slowing as usual. He was drawn back out a few minutes later when something felt amiss.

Myrskyr shifted uncomfortably. He didn't see the point of meditating when there were more interesting things to do and learn. He closed his eyes as instructed but his mind was alive with questions, new and old that he wanted answered. He opened them and stared around the shrine out of boredom and then at Kittal. He was astonished to see that Kittal had risen off the floor of the cave but already he was descending. His eyes didn't open as with a sigh he said, "I know you think this is pointless but believe me when I say it will help. I also was once an angry young man."

"Why?" Myrskyr eagerly asked to delay the meditating. Kittal pursed his lips together as he frowned, "it is not for now. Now is about you, not me. Now, close your eyes and concentrate." He opened one eye to check the young God was doing as he was told.

With a heavy sigh Myrskyr did as he was told.

Satisfied Kittal returned to his own meditating.

Myrskyr frowned in his concentration. He tried to calm his mind and was surprised when his thoughts went blank. They weren't for long as soon he was hearing voices and he recognised them as his brothers. He demanded, *"show yourselves cowards!"*

"Look at our brother, all human." One of them sneered.

"I'm one of you." He declared, *"I'll prove it."*

With a roar he changed into a dragon and he shouted, *"let me back in the Heavens."*

"No!" There was a flash of lightning out of the darkness and it hit Myrskyr.

He felt the raw energy flow through him but was paralysed to the spot as well. He roared in frustration, *"what have I done?!"*

"The fall must have knocked your head." The first voice laughed.

"I am your brother."

"You betrayed us." The second voice said accusingly.

"Say it to my face." He snarled.

     Kittal knew there was something wrong when the black clouds looming over his garden of tranquillity descended as a thick fog and then he was thrown out by a force that threw him against something hard. Opening his eyes he found himself against the wall of the cave and the cave itself filled with the body of a dark purple dragon. Its tail stuck out of the cave, twitching, and he was trapped by a hind leg. He saw the scar on the dragon's shoulder and realised it was Myrskyr. He shoved at the leg and shouted, *"Myrskyr!"*

He had to cover his ears as a boom of thunder filled what little space there was left in the cave. As the thunder faded he called out again, *"Myrskyr! Come back to me."*

     The hind leg shifted and Kittal scrambled on to the dragon before he became trapped again, ignoring the pain from his bruised back. He prayed that Myrskyr wouldn't arch his back otherwise he would hit the ceiling of the cave. He moved quickly along the curved length of the dragon using the feathery mane. He felt Myrskyr shift under him and froze. The dragon settled.

     He needed to get into Myrskyr's mind. He worried he had done the wrong thing in getting the God to meditate but he needed him to be able to control himself. He wouldn't be able to trust him until he could control his changes.

     Reaching the God's neck he buried his hands into the

feathery mane so dark that is was almost black except when the light caught it and it turned purple, and pressed against the nerve that would hopefully bring him to his senses. He closed his eyes and hoped he could pull Myrskyr with him to his garden. Already he was regretting not telling the young man.

Myrskyr cried out in sudden pain. It felt as if every muscle in his body was seizing. He heard his brothers laughing somewhere in the darkness and wanted to kill them. He growled, wanting to charge them but he felt himself being pulled away. He felt a weight on the back of his neck but couldn't turn his head to snap at it. He couldn't stop himself being pulled away from the voices of his brothers.

Suddenly he was in a garden, destroying shrubs and scattering flowers as he thrashed in protest. He saw children wailing and clinging to a woman who stood her ground. He heard a new voice sternly say, *"can you try not to destroy my garden and scare my wife and children."*
Myrskyr turned his head and saw Kittal with his hands buried in his mane concentrating on staying on. Kittal stared grimly at Myrskyr, *"you wanted to know my peaceful place, well, here you are."*

Myrskyr became still as he looked round and saw the destruction he had wrought. The children and woman had disappeared. He felt guilty that Kittal had had to drag him to his private place and then he had destroyed it in seconds and all Kittal had been trying to do was help him. He began to shrink and Kittal slipped off his back. Before long he was a young man again. He whispered, "I'm sorry."

"It's all right. I'll enjoy regrowing it all. Where did you go?" Kittal ended with concern.

"I did as you said..." Myrskyr began but got distracted as the garden was already beginning to regrow, shrubs growing bushy again, broken flower stems growing buds and blooming. The one thing that didn't change was the oppressive black clouds. Kittal saw him looking and remarked, "that's because of you."

"Oh."

"Now, what happened?"

133

Returning his attention back to the Nejus Myrskyr said, "I tried to empty my mind of all thoughts and then there was voices, my brothers mocking me and I got angry. I'm sorry."

"What did they say?"

"That I betrayed them."

"Can you remember what you did for them to accuse you like that?" Kittal frowned.

"No."

"Don't worry about it now but we do need to think of a place where they can't get to you."

"I can think of one place but rather not use it."

"Go on?"

Myrskyr gulped, "the palace in Bakamon. They couldn't find me there but I have lots of memories I'd rather forget."

"What about when you were with Zhina? Use that." Kittal suggested, "it doesn't have to be exactly like the palace. Make it your own. My garden doesn't look like this." He paused and then remarked, "I think we've had enough for today."

"I have disturbed your own meditation."

"Don't worry. We'll try again tomorrow." Kittal smiled reassuringly at the young man.

Twenty-One

Tania's pregnancy progressed and by the third trimester she found herself able to stomach more than just plain bread and her father's infusion. She was determined to give birth to the child growing inside her and not feel like a complete failure and honour the promise she had given her father in never trying again. She also wanted him to see her fit and strong again so he wouldn't worry about her when he returned to the Valley.

A part of her loved having her father near though there were times he was distracted. She knew she was just another item on his list of concerns along with the God and his two companions, Lulizen, Ozanus and his own person. She felt sure there were new worry lines on his forehead as well as laughter lines in the corners of his eyes.

Sometimes as she caught old age creeping up on him she wished she had been born a man so she could shoulder some of his responsibilities. At other times she was proud of how much strength, physically and mentally, he had to keep going especially when she watched him training with the Suwars.

She was not the only one watching. Gaexon and Myrskyr watched secretly from their spot on the wall with awe and jealousy. They felt sure Kittal knew they were there but as he never said anything they continued to pretend he didn't know they watched. Myrskyr knew he would never be invited to join the Suwars in practice as it was bad enough trying to control himself when he got angry. He didn't want to think what might happen if he was allow to fight even if it was only practising.

Currently Kittal was still taking him to his garden. Neither knew what would happen if Myrskyr tried to meditate by himself again. He saw a different side to Kittal. He saw the family man with three young children and not just the stern but fair ruler.

Gaexon watched the practices wistfully. He wanted to be down there as well. He had even approached Harim who had laughed at him, "only those with the blood of the Suwars can become one."

"What about Diego?" Gaexon challenged.

"That is a rarity. That started as a punishment for Joli. Now go away."

Gaexon had had to walk away frustrated.

Zhina had joined them a few times to watch but then had grown quickly bored. She had wanted her and Myrskyr to be like before but he didn't need her to look after him anymore. He didn't need her making sure he ate as he ate eagerly and hungrily. His body filled out and grew muscular.

And he had Gaexon. She still wasn't sure of him. She felt sure he had other motives but didn't know what they were. Maybe it was because the two young men hung out together all the time apart from when Myrskyr was with Kittal and she felt left out.

Thankfully Tania took her in and her urge to look after someone, anyone, transferred to Kittal's pregnant daughter who enjoyed the company. Zhina was glad to feel needed but still she got distracted with thoughts of Myrskyr.

Kittal was out by the barracks with Harim and Canaan when a muddy green dragon with a forked tail circled overhead and then landed. The dragon was breathing heavily, panting clouds of steam. Kittal approached with a frown as the Suwar slipped off and unwrapped the turban. Sternly he said, "you have pushed your dragon too hard Suwar."

"Nejus." The Suwar pressed a fist to her chest in salute, "the Nejusana has given birth."

"Boy or girl?" He demanded, forgetting he had been concerned for the dragon moments earlier.

"Boy sir." The dragon declared between breaths.

The Suwar turned on the dragon, *"who was sent as messenger?"*

136

"Oh come on, we can both enjoy being the one delivering good news."
Kittal instantly felt torn. He wanted to see Lulizen and see she was well and see his new son but he had promised to stay in Jukir till Tania either birthed or lost her child. Harim made the decision for him, "go, you need to name him."
"Tania is doing well. She won't be upset if you went." Canaan added.

Kite had already seen the new dragon and knew something was a foot. From the hillside where the dragons roosted she flew down and landed on the barracks so the new dragon knew who was more senior. She demanded, *"what is happening?"*

"Get down here Kite, we must go home for a few days." Kittal beamed up at her as Canaan headed into the barracks to get her saddle. He turned to Harim, "can you watch Myrskyr, he still can't control himself and you might need to calm him. I know you've done it before."
"Of course."
"Thank you."
Kite landed and folded her wings in as Canaan came out with her saddle. She was excited for the journey as she hadn't flown a long distance for a while. When she had first learnt her Nejus had gone with the sea dragons she had spent several days challenging herself, determined to cross the sea and bring him back but reluctantly she had to admit defeat as she wore herself out and then slept for two days, curled up to preserve what little heat and energy she had left.

Canaan handed the saddle to Kittal and the older man threw it on to Kite's back as he said, "Canaan can you fetch me my coat and headscarf? There is no time to change."
He wanted to be there before the next day was out. He knew that she wasn't alone but this was not the time to leave her. She would expect him otherwise the Suwar wouldn't have been sent and he wanted to be there. He needed to name the child.

Within the hour he and Kite were in the air flying over the sea between Jukirla and its sister port of Senspanta and then over the cliffs where they had all camped six years previously to

137

free the dragons of Jukirla. They stopped only as the sun began to set. Kittal ate the small parcel of bread and cheese thrown to him by Harmin before curling up in the safety of Kite's curled tail.

Both instinctively woke as dawn broke. Kittal stood and stretched before climbing back into his saddle. He wasn't going to push Kite but he knew she could feel his own urgency in wanting to get to their valley home.

Lulizen sat on the veranda with her long black hair in a single plait and dressed in a loose gown and a shawl over her shoulders. Her two daughters sat at her feet on cushions while Ozanus was on the lawn with Da'ud beginning his training with a sword in the cool of the evening. The four day old in her arms was wrapped in a worn red blanket that had grown thin in places and patched in others for it had been used by many generations to name the children of the Nejus. She knew her husband would show up tonight.

There was a shout from the edge of the lawn and everyone looked up. Silhouetted against the red sky was a dragon, wings spread wide as it spiralled downwards. With a thrill in her heart Lulizen stood and approached the top of the steps. Da'ud grabbed Ozanus and pulled him off the lawn as Arno ran across it. Seconds later Kite landed with a roar that was echoed by the others in their nests on the valley's cliffs.

Ozanus was in awe of his father as he always was every time he saw him land. He stared with his hand still in Da'ud's from fighting his grip. Da'ud's grip loosened and he escaped to run towards his father who had just slipped off Kite's back. A smile filled his face which fell as Kittal barely brushed a hand through the boy's hair as his eyes and direction of travel were set firmly on Lulizen and his new son. Ozanus was crestfallen and glared at the baby.

Kittal strode up the four steps and swept Lulizen and child into his arms. She laughed, "careful, you'll wake him." He drew up her face and pressed his lips hard against hers just as the baby let out a wail from being squashed between his parents. Kittal reluctantly broke away as Lulizen smiled, "I told you so."

138

Sobering he said, "I can't stay for long."

"How is Tania doing?"

"Very well, but I am here for you."

"Here." She pressed the grizzling baby into his arms, "he has been waiting for his name."

He nodded.

"Be careful out there."

"I will be. Arno, a lantern please."

"Sir." Arno eagerly lit one of several lamps that lived by the top of the steps.

"Ozanus!" Kittal turned and called.

"Papa?" Ozanus appeared, warily eyeing his baby brother.

"Come. You can have your first lesson in being Nejus. Hold on to Arno's hand." Kittal said sternly, "you'll see what you need to do when you have your own children to name."

To Ozanus that felt like it would be a long time but if it meant he got precious time with his father he wasn't going to say no. He took Arno's held out hand and allowed Arno to lead him through the vegetation with father and new son behind them.

The Dragon Lord's shrine was bathed in the last of the red light from the setting sun, just enough time for Kittal to present his new son to the god. He held up his son to the hole in the ceiling, "O Lord let me present my new son."

"Name him." A voice spoke frightening Ozanus who stood by his father's side.

"Ioan."

"Bring him up well for he will be there to support his brother."

"Thank you O Lord." Kittal smiled as he drew his son back to his chest and looked down at Ozanus. Gently he said, "don't be afraid. I did this with you as well and Kite's daughter was named for you just as Kite is named for me."

"I don't think I will remember." Ozanus admitted.

Kittal crouched down to be the same height as his son, "I just wanted you to see and hear. Do you know who spoke?"

"Our Dragon Lord."

"That's right." Kittal smiled and Ozanus smiled with pride as well, "and he said Ioan would be there to support you in the future so you won't be alone, you'll have him helping you but

139

first you'll have to help him."

"Why?" Ozanus demanded with a frown.

"You are his big brother so while he can't defend himself you must protect him. I am only here for a day, so will you look after your mother, sisters and new brother for me?"

"When are you coming home?"

Kittal sighed for he wanted to be home as well. All he could say was, "soon."

He didn't want to promise anything to his son that he might not be able to keep. Ozanus frowned but accepted the answer.

"Shall we go back and tell mama the name of your baby brother?"

Ozanus nodded and took hold of the hand his father held out. Kittal led them out of the shrine to where Arno waited, "lead the way young man."

Arno bowed his head and then headed back down the path.

In the half hour they had been away the two girls had gone reluctantly to bed. Lulizen remained on the veranda for all of her men to return. She smiled with relief as they all appeared. Ozanus broke away and ran to her and announced excitedly, "he is called Ioan. The Dragon Lord spoke to us."

"Did he now?" She smiled at her son and rested a hand on his head but her eyes were fixed on her husband and their new son. He squirmed and tugged at her sleeve, "mama, mama?"

She looked down, "what Ozanus?"

Ozanus fell silent as he realised he didn't have her full attention. He turned and glared at his father and baby brother. He could share his parents' love with his sisters because they were girls and silly things but he didn't want to share it with another brother. He wanted to be their only son again, their special boy even though he had just agreed to protect him.

His sisters' nursemaid appeared and Lulizen said softly, "time for bed."

"But papa…?" Ozanus turned back to look at his mother.

"Not tonight Ozanus." She answered sternly and with a sulky pout he crossed to the nursemaid and allowed her to guide him into the house. He fought the tears he could feel stinging his eyes. He could already see that his mother was losing interest in

140

him. He wanted to run back and wrap himself round her legs and cry and scream and demand that Ioan get sent away and return to where he had come from, wherever that was, but he reminded himself he was a big boy and beginning to learn how to use a sword unlike the baby. He smiled at that thought.

Kittal handed Ioan over as the infant's arms wiggled out of the blanket and he began to whimper. Lulizen smiled, "he's probably hungry again." She held out a hand, "come to bed while I feed him."

"I should see Rafferty." Kittal reluctantly said.

"Not tonight." She decided, "tonight you are mine. He can see you before you go back to Jukir. Tell me everything that has happened to you."

Once in their bedroom Kittal told her about everything that had happened to him apart from being raped by the Empress. As he ended and she lay Ioan in the cradle carved with dragons. She asked, "is it wise to bring a dragon who can't control himself to this Valley? I know he's a God and we need to help him but would he be safe around our children?"

"I'm working on it." He answered as Lulizen slipped under the sheets and snuggled against him. He absent-mindedly kissed the top of her head as he thought about all there was to do before he could come back.

He slept in later than planned. He slept through Ioan crying for food and to be changed and the children squabbling outside his door. He woke mid-morning when Arno shook him awake, "sir, your tea is ready."
Groggily Kittal sat up, "what time is it?"

"Late morning sir."

"Damn it." Kittal swung his legs out of bed and Arno hurried to get his clothes, "I'll have breakfast in my study."

"It's already in there and so is Rafferty."

"Thank you Arno."
Looking at the young man Kittal was impressed with how he was turning out. He was becoming just as good as Canaan apart from being unable to speak the dragon language. He hadn't managed to get his tongue round it all yet and could just about

141

fetch Kite for him.

Arno smiled with pride at having pleased his Nejus.

Kittal walked through to his study where Rafferty sat at his Nejus' desk till he saw Kittal enter, "welcome back sir."

"You have about two hours of me and then I have to go again."

"There's more than that." Rafferty exclaimed.

"Just give me the important bits that can't wait. I have to get back to Jukirla and hopefully see my grandchild born before I can return." Kittal explained as he sat down and picked up his steaming bowl of his special tea and sipped at it. Rafferty shifted through the pile of papers and found the first one.

Three hours later Kittal had dealt with various reports, pleads for justice, advice on punishments and organised for his Suwars to investigate suspicious activity near the western border. He set the man up to organise a tour of the towns of Keytel with brief excursions to visit allies. Rafferty grumbled at the work but became silent when his Nejus reminded him there were two of them to handle the work.

With the administration of running a country and growing family dealt with Kittal sent Arno to fetch Kite while he went to find Lulizen. He found her asleep in a chair while the children's nursemaid softly sung to Ioan. He crouched down and ran a hand over her cheek. She sighed and pressed against his calloused hand and slowly opened her eyes. Softly he said, "it's time."

"Already?" She sighed.

"Just another month and then I'll be back."

"Tell Tania I'm praying for her."

"I will." He put his hand under her chin drew her face closer to his so he could kiss her.

Before he could there was a scream. They both rose and looked out as Kite flew down with Arno in one of her foreclaws, screaming. Kittal ran out, *"Kite?! What do you think you are doing?!"*

"He needs to show more respect," she complained as she dropped Arno, *"and learn our language."*

"He finds it hard." Kittal said as he helped his servant up, "what did you say to her?"

142

"Just that you were ready to return to Jukirla." Arno answered wide eyed and shaking.

"Are you hurt?"

"I don't think so."

"I'll talk to her. She's never done this before." He frowned with concern.

Arno nodded before saying, "I'll get your saddle and coat." He glanced briefly at the scowling dragon before running across the lawn and into the house.

With hands on hips Kittal demanded, *"what were you playing at?"*

"Everyone is afraid."

"Of what? What have you been telling them?"

"Can you not feel it?"

"Feel what?"

"When I am near that God I feel angrier. I want to fight. We are afraid of what it will do to us in our home."

"He's got to come back here where I can help him."

"He fell from the heavens so he must be able to fly up there by now."

"His brothers won't let him."

"He's a God. He has to try." She looked pleadingly at him, *"I fear what will happen to this world while he remains down here."*

Kittal was thoughtful for a moment before saying, *"all right we'll give it a go but I'll need your help."*

She nodded with relief.

"But you still need to apologise to Arno. That is not acceptable behaviour for a dragon, especially mine. Do you want to become your mother?"

She bowed her head and grunted. That was the closest he would get as an agreement. He eyed her sternly, *"here he comes."*

"Arno, I apologise."

Kittal nodded encouragingly at the young man who looked warily at his Nejus' dragon. He gulped and then carefully said, *"thank you."*

"I'm glad we are all friends again." Kittal remarked brightly as he took the saddle from Arno.

143

Kittal growled but stopped when she saw Kittal glaring at her and rolled her eyes instead.

Twenty-Two

The air was tense around the island of Jukirla as they reached it. Kittal stood in his saddle peering ahead with a frown. Black clouds circled the large island with streaks of lightning flashing through them. He realised that Kite was right, nothing would be right in this world until the God was back in the heavens. The God grew stronger and one day he wouldn't be able to control him. So far the meditating hadn't helped.

They flew through the clouds, narrowly missing being hit by a fork of lightning. Kittal shouted, *"I'm doing what our Lord asked me to do! You can't stop me!"*
There were growls from within the clouds and Kittal and Kite caught each other's eye. Silently she acknowledged his apology. She knew he had a lot of other worries, many of them human and that he wasn't as observant to the lives of dragons anymore. She decided she would try harder to let him know in the future but firstly they needed the Thunder God back in the heavens where he belonged.

Breaking through the clouds there was a roar that sounded like thunder. Three dragons tumbled through the air before them, broke apart and two of them flapped their wings. A dark red one rose in front of them, a spiney ball of bone at the end of its tail followed by his brother. Between them twisting his serpentine body was Myrskyr. The God opened his mouth and a rumble of thunder came from it as he then snapped at the brothers. The first swung his tail and it hit Myrskyr in the side who fell before recovering. He streaked upwards, back claw extended and scored the thick scales of the second.

The three moved around Kite and Kittal as if they were

an obstacle to manoeuvre around. Kite roared, hoping the mate
of their leader would break them from the spell they were under.
They either didn't hear it or ignored it. Kittal shouted,
"Myrskyr!"
The God turned and saw Kittal and realised he was in serious
trouble but he hadn't been able to stop it. He had wanted a fight
and there had been dragons willing to. He was knocked sideways
as the tail of one of the brother's slammed into him. The dragon
frowned as Myrskyr didn't retaliate. It turned and saw its Nejus
and its heart sank.

   "Colomoball!" Kittal shouted in anger, a name that had stuck
as his rider hadn't been able to pronounce his name when
younger.
Colomoball's brother, a sandy dragon with a large bony crest,
shot upwards, head lowered to head-butt Myrskyr in the
stomach, unaware that the other two were now hovering in the
air. Myrskyr was forced upwards, stunned, body bending before
beginning to fall, changing into a man as he did. Kittal shouted,
"Kite, get him! Colomoball get ready to catch me."
        Kittal jumped out of his saddle as Kite dived to catch the
falling god. Colomoball swooped under his falling Nejus who
landed with a grunt on the dragon's neck. Angry with all three of
them Kittal said, *"I will talk to all of you later. Lets all get safely
to the ground first."*
Nevis was shaking his head to clear his spinning sight after
hitting Myrskyr and realised the fight had come to a sudden end.
He saw Kittal on his brother's back, *"Nejus?!*

   "This has ended." Kittal growled, *"we are going down, now!"*
Nevis' head shrank into his neck in shame and turned to head
down. Kite swooped up, Myrskyr clinging to her back, so that
Kittal could see he was safe before turning to circle downwards.

        Landing on the ground and Nevis on the barracks the
three of them looked sheepish and covered in bloody grazes and
cuts, as Kittal stood before them and demanded, *"what do you
think you were playing at? You two,"* looking at Colomoball and
Nevis, *"should know better and you,"* looking at Myrskyr who
shifted uncomfortably beside Kite, *"what happened to
restraining yourself? Has all that training gone to waste? I don't*
146

want to hear anything from any of you at the moment."
He saw Nevis' mouth open and then it shut as he carried on, *"I expect an explanation and apology from each of you later. Now go before I add to your wounds."*
Myrskyr ran to the Governor's House while Colomoball and Nevis rose into the air.

Once alone Kittal drew in a deep breath, there were times when the dragons behaved worst than his children and this was one of them and two of them should have known better. Calming he approached Kite as Diego also appeared to help him get the saddle off Kite. Diego asked, "what just happened?"

"I don't want to talk about it." Kittal responded sharply. Diego looked to Kite but she shook her head. If her Nejus didn't want to talk about, guessing by the tone of his voice, then neither would she. Diego frowned but didn't push either of them as he was sure to hear something in the next few hours. Taking him by surprise Kittal said, "get Katerina and Mexica to see to their dragons."

"Yes sir." Diego puffed as Kite's saddle was dumped into his arms. He lingered as Kittal walked away as Canaan appeared, "Nejus?"

"Not now." Kittal growled.

"Myrskyr is covered in cuts and grazes like he has been in a fight." Canaan persisted as he turned and hurried to keep up with his leader.

"Why did no one try to stop them?" Kittal demanded.

"Stop what?"
Myrskyr stepped into view just inside the house, "Kittal? Sir?"

"Not now Myrskyr. Go get yourself cleaned up and maybe then I will see you." Kittal remarked sternly.
Canaan nodded and gave the God a tight smile.

"I want food, a bath and some clean clothes." Kittal demanded.

"Already being sorted."
Kittal visibly relaxed then, glad that Canaan was around to keep everything running smoothly.

Myrskyr crept into the bedroom, bandages wrapped round the worst of the claw cuts and in clean clothes. The room

147

was in darkness from the curtains being drawn, apart from one lit lamp on the desk and he wondered if the Nejus was ill. As he had passed through the house he had heard worried mutterings from the servants and knew it was his fault. He had already made the decision he had to try and get to the heavens and wanted to tell Kittal.

Kittal came into view, dressed in his usual tunic, sash and trousers, in the lamplight, "yes?"

"I'm sorry, really sorry." Once again the unsure young man.

"Hmpfh. Not good enough." Kittal sat down at the table.

"Zhina tried to stop me but when the clouds appeared yesterday all I wanted to do was fight…. Sir?"
Kittal looked up from the papers he had brought with him from the Valley to look through, "yes?"

"I think I'm strong enough to try. I know I'm starting to affect everything. The other two wouldn't have fought if it wasn't for me. I will take the punishment." Myrskyr puffed out his chest. Kittal curtly nodded, "get your strength back up and then we will try."

"And Colomoball and Nevis?"

"They will still need to be punished. They should have been disciplined enough to refuse you." Kittal answered stiffly and then returned to his papers.

Myrskyr took the hint and left and found Gaexon standing outside who exclaimed, "are you insane?! He could have chosen not to help you anymore."

"I know. I've apologised."

"If you have that need to fight again come and find me and we'll wrestle as men, then I can make sure it doesn't get out of hand." Gaexon said, a little more calmly as they headed down the corridor.

"I'm going to try in the next day or so." Myrskyr told his friend.

"Try what?"

"To return to the heavens so that everyone stops being angry and the black clouds will go away." Myrskyr explained, eager to be able to tell someone other than the Nejus his decision.

"Wow." Gaexon looked surprised and didn't know what to say.
148

Finally he asked, "and if it doesn't work?"

"Then we can find out what I need to do to get up there."

In his bedroom Kittal sighed over his papers, a headache sitting at the back of his eyes so he was struggling to read. He had never really been one for headaches but since arriving back at Jukirla one had formed. The pressure in his mind was oppressive and he felt sure it wasn't a natural headache. He squeezed his eyes shut and sent a silent pray to the Dragon Lord that Myrskyr would successfully return to the heavens before any more fights could occur. He gave up on the papers and went to lie on his bed and hoped a few hours sleep would rid him of the headache.

Twenty-Three

Canaan, Diego and Harim stood to one side of the scuffed dirt yard while their Nejus' checked Kite's saddle. They glanced at Myrskyr who stood nearby with his two companions. None of them were sure how successful it was going to be especially as the black clouds hanging over them looked even denser than they had been the last few days and the humidity and static was growing. They all hoped that it would be successful so that life could return to normal and Kittal could stop being distracted by the God.

Kittal, dressed in borrowed dragon hide armour, leather sewn together to look like dragon scales, as he didn't know what he was going to come up against, called out to Myrskyr, "ready?"

Myrskyr glanced over before accepting a hug from Zhina. Feeling her pressed against him he felt a rush of blood to his groin. He found his human mind telling him to stay on the ground and discover more about this sudden new feeling especially as Zhina had filled out, including her breasts which he had seen others eyeing, and her short hair framed her attractive face which smiled shyly at him now. She softly said, "look down at me sometimes." She held one of his hands and gave it a squeeze.

He turned to Gaexon, "thank you."

"Good luck."

"And you in whatever you do."

They grinned at each other. Gaexon reached out and patted his friend on the shoulder. Myrskyr frowned as he saw a wistfulness in the other's eyes that he didn't understand. What was Gaexon

150

hiding from him? It was too late to find out now as Kittal called for him again. He looked at the two people he never thought he could call friends and said, "thank you for everything you've done for me."

Before they could persuade him to stay he ran across the yard to where Kittal and Kite stood. Kittal frowned as he studied the young man, "ready?"
Myrskyr nodded.

"Kite is coming with us, as high as she can get to catch me when it's time for me to get off." He didn't want to think of the complaints his body would make when he landed heavily on her, "in your own time."
He retreated to give Myrskyr space to grow and morph into his dragon form.

With a slow deep breath Myrskyr concentrated on changing. He hoped it would work as at all other times he had been angry or frustrated. He felt a hand on his shoulder and felt energy course through him from Kittal. With a gasp of surprise he dropped to his knees and fell forward on to his hands as he felt his back arch and stretch.

First his back grew to its scaly dragon length and then the human coccyx bone grew into his tail. His legs and arms grew large muscles and the feet and hands became his hind and fore claws. A feathery mane pushed its way through his skin like pins through thick fabric. Finally his face began to change, forming a long snout with wide nostrils and whiskers that dropped pass his long jaw. His new mouth filled with sharp teeth and he gnashed them.

Forgetting where he was he roared and thunder rumbled around the yard as if the storm was above their heads. There was a corresponding crack of lightning which streaked across the clouds as multiply forks of electricity. Kittal looked up as the sound of thunder dissipated and feared for himself and Kite. He knew Myrskyr as the Thunder God would be able to handle it as an immortal being but neither him nor Kite were immortal.

Myrskyr turned large eyes that were like black abysses on Kittal, *"ready?"*
Kittal climbed on and dug his hands into the God's mane and
151

hoped his day of deep meditation would be enough of a boost for the God to reach the heavens, *"let's do this before your brothers try to stop us."*

Myrskyr looked intently skyward, thinking only of his home in the sky as he twisted upwards, using his immortal powers to send him soaring towards the clouds. The black clouds shifted and blue sky could be seen above, teasing him. Kittal knew Myrskyr would only have seconds to get through and shouted, *"faster! Faster!"*

Myrskyr whipped his tail and his whole body leapt upwards towards the clear blue sky. Lightning streaked after them as the clouds began to close back up behind the three of them. Kite roared as a bolt of lightning caught the end of her tail and singed it.

Out from the oppressive atmosphere around Jukirla Myrskyr and Kite hovered catching their breaths. Kittal found himself grinning, *"we did it."*

Kite and Myrskyr found themselves laughing, joining in the man's exuberance.

"The next step is to go even higher." Myrskyr remarked as they stopped laughing.

Kite and Kittal looked upwards with trepidation. This next step could potentially kill any one of them or even both of them. They looked at each other, both accepting they had had a good life and though they had families who would miss them they knew they wouldn't be forgotten.

"Ready?" Myrskyr remembered to ask while intently staring upwards. He had to keep reminding himself that he was not alone.

"Lets go." Kittal said, bracing himself. He dug his numb hands deeper into Myrskyr's mane and closed his eyes, concentrating all the powers he had as the High Priest in his hands and directing them towards the God's heart and muscles.

Myrskyr circled a few times and then began to lazily spiral upwards, conserving his energy for one big burst as he sensed himself nearing home.

Kittal felt himself becoming light-headed and found it harder and harder to breath. Just before he lost consciousness he said, *"I don't want to see you ever again."*

"Thank you for all your help." Myrskyr answered as he felt the man slip from him. He whipped his tail and sensed home. Now was the time to use the additional energies given to him by Kittal. With a roar he sped up but came to a sudden stop. A weight held him back, an invisible line seemed to be anchoring him to the ground. He squirmed and wiggled like a fish on a hook. He roared in frustration as he began to be pulled down.

Far below him Kittal fell and Kite caught him, dropping through the air herself from the uncontrollable speed. She folded her wings around her rider to protect him from the up-draft threatening to draw him away from her. Feeling him stir and weakly grab hold of the girth of her saddle she spread her wings to slow their descent.

She looked up when she heard a boom of thunder filled with frustration and knew the attempt had failed. Her Nejus had given his all and it hadn't been enough and now they were stuck with an angry frustrated God. She didn't want him near her Valley home where he would easily influence the youngsters, including her own; but she knew she had no say. As she slowly descended in wide sweeping circles she glanced behind and saw Kittal slowly blinking away tears from the cold air. Hoarsely he asked, *"did we do it?"*
She didn't hear his question.

Within the centre of her circling Myrskyr flew straight down, intent on revenge. He smashed through the top layers of cloud and roared, *"show yourselves!"*
He could sense his brothers nearby.

"Fight or are you cowards!"
They sprang out of the darkness, claws sharp and teeth bared.

On the ground it began to rain, a few drops at first and then a downpour which quickly soaked everyone to the skin that got caught in it. Rain poured down the sloping streets, topping doorsteps and seeping into houses. Exclamations of terror were made as the population of Jukirla ran for cover and slammed doors, windows and shutters to keep out the rain. They feared the world was coming to an end. The dragons looked to the sky and hoped Myrskyr had made it and was extracting his revenge and

153

then the blue sky would return. They adjusted their wings so the rain ran off them and protected the few Suwars who were with them.

Tania's baby chose this time of fear to come into the world. She didn't even know that her father was involved as Canaan had promised not to tell. With the midwife and Zhina close at hand she screamed out her pain and crushed the sheets in clenched fists until she was forced on to the birthing stool, the sheet trailing behind her. Zhina wiped the sweat from her brow with a damp cloth as with a long whining moan the baby slipped from Tania, two weeks early.

Silence filled the room as the three women held their breaths waiting for the first mew of life from the bloody infant. There was a cry of protest at being expelled from its warm watery cocoon. The midwife lifted the child up and wrapped it in an old blanket and cleaned its nose, mouth and eyes before handing it to the shaking Tania who asked, "is it real?"

The midwife smiled, "yes. Now I will cut the umbilical cord and get the afterbirth expelled."

Afraid that the babe would suddenly die she didn't dare to hold it, "give it to Zhina."

Zhina was completely surprised to be suddenly holding the new born and struggled to hold it at first. She stared down at the wrinkly red-faced wailing baby in her arms. The midwife instructed, "hold her close so she can feel your heart."

Zhina held the baby girl close to her and a feeling of warmth and of love for small defenceless babes swept through her. She realised she had missed the chance to have Myrskyr's children if that would have even been possible.

"She?" Tania tentatively asked as the midwife pressed down on her exposed swollen stomach.

"Yes, a girl." The midwife glanced up to check Tania's reaction. So many wives wanted the all important heir and were disappointed when they birthed a daughter. She knew Tania should just be grateful that she had finally birthed a child at all. She felt a contraction and the afterbirth spilt out, thankfully complete. She pulled Tania up, "time for you to rest. I'll clean

154

the babe and let your husband know and then it will be time to feed her." She glanced at her assistant and saw that Zhina glowed with love for the girl. Clearly this had been the first time Zhina had seen the miracle of life blessed upon all women and some day she would get to experience the pain and love for herself.

Through half closed eyes Tania said, "please offer the afterbirth to the Gods in thanks."

"Of course. Now sleep." The midwife said as she pressed a pad of cotton between Tania's thighs to slow the flow of blood as the womb started the process of cleansing itself.

"And Canaan….?"

"I will tell him."

"And father…?"

"Of course I will." The midwife carefully said but Tania had already fallen asleep.

After cleaning the baby the midwife left Zhina to watch over mother and child to seek out the father. She found Canaan with Diego, Harim and Gaexon in the garden, soaking wet but unable to move, eyes fixed on the sky. It had been hours since their Nejus and the two dragons had headed skyward. The clouds swirled menacingly, and thunder boomed out as lightning flashed within, briefly lighting up the clouds revealing four shapes within. At another flash three of the serpentine shapes had moved while the fourth looked recognisably like a dragon from earth. She hesitated, trying to decide which was more important. She decided that his new child was more so and tapped him on the shoulder, "sir?"

So intently was he watching that he jumped and spun round, hand going to the knife at his belt. He relaxed and tensed again as he saw it was the skilled midwife watching over Tania. With a voice edged with fear he asked, "what's wrong?"

She smiled at him, glad to be bringing him good news, "mother **and daughter** are doing well."

He looked stunned, he didn't even know Tania had gone into labour.

Diego and Harim had turned to find out what was going on. Catching the midwife's words they both broke into grins and

155

patted Canaan on the back. Canaan looked round at them and found the grins to be infectious as he declared in disbelief, "I'm finally a father."

"And we really are pleased for you." Harim remarked with pleasure. He hoped that Canaan and Tania would be reunited in their new family life.

The joyous moment was interrupted by Gaexon, "look!" All three of them turned to where the charcoal burner pointed. Within the flashes of lightning they saw one of the Gods collide with the dragon. The dragon faltered and began to fall while struggling to stay in flight, clearly exhausted. The dragon managed to recover but none of them knew for how long it could stay aloft.

Within the flash of another streak of lightning they saw one of the Gods pushed out of the cloud backwards and begin to fall as well. The God turned into a man as it fell and landed with a splash into the yard that had become a giant mud pool. The rain stopped, the lightning died and the clouds stopped moving.

Gaexon broke away from the group, knowing who it would be. He ran through the house calling Zhina's name till she appeared with a frown, "what?"

"It failed. He's just crash landed."

Zhina glanced at mother and daughter who were finally united after Tania had found the courage to hold her child and now clung to her as the child snuffled for milk. Her loyalties returned to Myrskyr and she abandoned them.

She ran with Gaexon out into the yard where they found Myrskyr lying spread eagled on his back staring up at the sky. They fell to their knees either side of him, calling out his name with growing fear.

Finally he blinked and they both breathed a sigh of relief, he was still alive. Zhina asked, "are you hurt?"

He thought that his pride was hurt more than anything but he also ached all over and now he had more new cuts over the ones that had only just scabbed over. He tried to sit up but fell backwards, back into the mud bath with a moan.

Gaexon and Zhina took an arm each and pulled him to his feet. They dragged him out of the yard and across the garden, his feet dragging through the mud and along the path. Others came to help as they reached the house and helped him to the room he shared with Gaexon.

As they passed through the garden Diego and Harim ran past, having sent Canaan to see mother and daughter. Now was not the time to be worrying about their Nejus when there were two other men who could.

They stood in the centre of the muddy yard watching Kite struggling to descend in a controlled manner. She was fighting exhaustion and keeping Kittal on her back. He was holding on by will power alone and giving her what little strength he had to help her reach the ground safely.

She tried to go for the barracks' roof ridge but missed and slid down the roof, taking tiles with her. She crashed to the ground, ripples forming in the puddles from the thud. Diego and Harim ran across and dragged Kittal clear before Kite turned on to her side and killed him with her weight. She managed to roll the other way creating a large hole in the wall of the barracks surprising several Suwars who had been inside.

Others came out of the door to stare at the scene. Never had any of them seen Kite be brought down before but here she was on her side gasping for breath as if her life depended upon it. She briefly lifted her head, *"Kit...?"*

"We have him." Harim said, *"just rest old girl. He would be proud of you."*

"I know." She tried to smile, *"is he...?"*

"Alive, yes, but don't know how alive." Harim said with a serious tone.

"Don't let him die."

"We will do our best."

"The God....?"

"Back with us. He landed just before you did." Diego answered as Kite's eyes rolled into the back of her head.

"How are we to move her?" A Suwar asked in the silence that fell.

"Leave her to rest and then she'll move herself." Harim said softly, "but lets build a bonfire to keep her warm."

Harim and Diego crouched beside their prone leader as

the Suwars gathered round them. One asked with fear, "is he alive?"

Diego glanced across at Harim, "whose your fastest Suwar? I think we should get the Nejusana here."

Whispers broke out amongst the Suwars. The Nejusana rarely left the Valley and if Diego wanted to bring her here then there was something seriously wrong with their High Chieftain.

"Katerina." Harim said, turning to look at her.

"On my way." She saluted and ran off to get changed and fetch her saddle.

Harim turned to two strong young Suwars, "help us get him to my rooms and then we can check him for broken bones."

"We should tell Tania." Diego pointed out.

"That is Canaan's job." Harim said sternly, "let him enjoy fatherhood for a bit first."

Once inside Kittal was laid on Harim's unmade bed that the Suwars smirked over till they received a glare. Now was not the time to be teasing their captain about his messy quarters when he expected them to keep theirs tidy. The only tidy area of the room was where his dragon-hide armour hung with pride. Harim growled, "you can go now and help make sure that bonfire is hot. We've got to keep Kite hot if we want her fire inside to stay alive."

Between Diego and Harim they stripped Kittal of the borrowed dragon hide armour. They carefully checked each arm and leg, his pelvis and turning him on his side they checked his back especially as there was no Delia to heal the damage this time. They deduced that at most their Nejus had broken a few ribs, the armour and turban having protected him from worst. He was cold to the touch so they built up a fire in the fireplace and covered the pale body in blankets and sat down to watch and wait. They'd never seen anything like it. It was almost like he was dead if it wasn't for his chest rising and falling.

Twenty-Four

Hearing the shouts Lulizen abandoned Rafferty and his papers to hurry outside. She watched as Nevis skidded to a stop on the lawn, creating deep gouges in the ground. She felt her heart tighten in her chest with fear, for a dragon not to land with its usual grace there had to be something wrong. She saw the slim figure of a Suwar slip out of the saddle and run across the lawn.

The Suwar fell on to one knee, "Nejusana, I'm here to take you to Jukirla."
Lulizen let out a howl of anguish and fell to her knees. She fought not to faint as servants ran out of the house. She knew one day it would happen but hoped for more warning. Damn the Dragon Lord! Damn the fallen God!

Tears rolled down her cheeks and then she saw three little faces staring at her, eyes wide with fear. The youngest whimpered, "mama?"
She beckoned them towards her and they ran and surrounded her and clung to her. She loved them more than ever now. They were all she had to remind her of Kittal.

An urgent voice broke through her grief. She looked up to see Arno standing beside the Suwar repeating himself, "madam? My lady? Madam..." He abruptly stopped when he saw she was now looking at him. Now he had her attention he said, "she says he was alive when she was sent to fetch you."
Lulizen gulped and turned to the Suwar, "I'll come, but I don't have anything suitable."

"I'll find you some bits from my lord's things." Arno piped up.

"And Ioan has to come too."

159

"I'll wrap him up so he's warm and get some cloth to make a sling." The nursemaid said.
The servants knew that their mistress needed to be with their master and she needed all problems taken away from her. They were quickly showing themselves to be capable servants in a time of crisis and Lulizen was silently grateful, "get…?"

"Katerina madam." The Suwar answered.

"Get Katerina something to eat and drink as she must be exhausted while I get changed."

Within the hour Lulizen was dressed in flying gear that smelt reassuringly of Kittal. She was grateful that the turban wrapped round her face hid her red eyes and tear-stained cheeks. Held pressed to her chest was Ioan wrapped up so only his little face peered silently up at her as if he knew something important was happening. Katerina instructed Nevis, *we carry our Nejusana now so we must ride fast but with care.*

"I understand."
Between the Suwar and the dragon Lulizen was helped up. Katerina sat behind her mistress and put an arm round her waist to steady her as the dragon rose into the air.

Though Lulizen wanted to demand that they keep going even she could feel that the dragon and its Suwar was tiring. They had had only an hour of rest. She fell asleep in the protective curl of the dragon's tail after feeding Ioan while Katerina kept watch, sword in its scabbard resting on her lap. Never had she thought she would have such a big responsibility and hoped she wouldn't mess it up.

It was with relief and aching muscles that Lulizen slipped from the dragon to find the barracks covered in scaffolding and Suwars hanging around the yard talking quietly. They all turned as the dragon landed and dropped down on one knee at the sight of their Nejusana. Harim appeared at the door of the barracks and beckoned her forward.

He bowed his head as she reached him, "madam."
As he lifted his head he had a nervous smile on his face, "he is awake and the doctor has seen him."
160

Though she wanted to see Kittal she also wanted to see the supposed God causing all the trouble she demanded as she unwrapped her borrowed headscarf, "where is this God then? How is Kite?"

Harim shifted uncomfortably as Myrskyr, though covered in cuts and bruises, was in a better state then Kittal who had only opened his eyes a few hours ago, "I can get him."

"Please, but first, where is my husband?"

"This way." He gestured inside the barracks.

She frowned, "why is he here and not at the house?"

"Because Tania doesn't know what has happened. We didn't want her to worry especially as she has just birthed her and Canaan's daughter."

Perhaps another time she would have turned and gone to Tania first but her husband needed her more. Harim led the way to his room where Kittal lay propped up, pale against the pillows, with a bandage wrapped round his chest.

His eyes were closed but they opened as he recognised Lulizen's footsteps. In disbelief he asked, "Luli?"

She smiled softly at him, "they came and got me. I thought you had died. Promise me, no more foolishness." She sat on the edge of the bed and undid the sling revealing a sleeping Ioan.

"You brought him with you?" He asked in surprise.

"Of course I did. What were you doing?" She had been told roughly what had happened but she wanted to hear it from her husband.

"I thought I had done it…. The higher you go the less air there is and the colder it gets, I lost consciousness. I gave him all I had and it wasn't enough." Kittal sighed.

There were footsteps in the corridor and Myrskyr burst through the door, slipping past Diego who tried to stop him. He came to a stop and stared. He could see what the failure had done to Kittal and suddenly felt guilty. Moments earlier he had been excited to see Kittal, having heard he had finally come round. He frowned at the woman holding a baby sat on the edge of the bed glaring at him.

She demanded of the young man with the shadows of bandages under his clothes, "and who might you be?"

161

"Nejusana, this is the Thunder God known as Myrskyr while with us." Harim replied with an emphasis on the first word as warning for Myrskyr.

She exclaimed, "you could have killed him!"

Trying to keep the peace Harim said, "he knew the risks."

"I don't care." She snapped at the Suwar. She turned back to the God and stood, "I don't want any excuses. If you really are a God then you should be able to get home without my husband's help."

Ioan started to whimper as he sensed the tension in the air. Myrskyr took a step backwards and Lulizen smirked, had he never seen an angry she-dragon out to protect her mate and offspring?

Diego and Harim stared. They had never seen this side of Lulizen.

Myrskyr's eyes were riveted to Lulizen's face and he was blushing in frustration and anger. Carefully he said as he tried to control himself, "I can't and I don't know why."

He felt his tight fists begin to change.

Diego and Harim looked from Myrskyr to Lulizen to see her reaction but she seemed immune. She had dealt with a fair few toddler tantrums now and just saw this as just another one and she knew how to deal with those. She dared him and before their eyes he deflated. He hung his head and murmured, "I'm sorry."

"I can't hear you."

Myrskyr looked up, "I'm sorry."

"Thank you. You may leave us."

Diego pulled Myrskyr from the room before any more damage was done. Clearly their Nejusana had taken a disliking to the young God and it was understandable.

Out in the corridor Zhina and Gaexon appeared, relieved to find Myrskyr who turned to Diego asking, "what did I do wrong?"

"You managed to offend a very worried Nejusana."

"How?"

Diego couldn't help smiling, "you have much to learn about women my friend." The smile slipped as he explained, "if our Lord had died that would have left us with a six-year-old Nejus

162

with no one to train him."

The three looked at each other and then Zhina asked the question no one dared ask, "will he live?"

"You sapped most of his life energy and power given to him by the Dragon Lord." Diego answered sternly. He glanced behind before adding, "look, you'd best go before she finds you here. I don't think any of us will be able to save you if she gets really angry. I don't think any of us have seen her that angry. Ever."

"Come on Myrskyr." Gaexon pulled Myrskyr by the arm. He didn't fancy meeting what sounded like a fiery woman.

Once outside Myrskyr shook off Gaexon's hand. He strode quickly away, ignoring Zhina's shout of concern. He quickly turned into a dragon and flew off. Kittal's meditating may not have worked but his powers bestowed on the man by the Dragon Lord had been enough to give him his full strength back.

He circled the island frustrated and confused. He had been so close and then had been dragged back down to the ground out of spite. He knew he could have done it. If only he knew what he had done wrong to offend his brothers but neither them nor the Dragon Lord were revealing anything. And now he had almost killed the one person who could help him and would he now want to continue helping him?

Then there were the confusing thoughts and emotions he was feeling and observing. He didn't like these human emotions. It felt like he had become more aware of them ever since he had escaped the palace. Without meaning to he had managed to offend an important person who was clearly going to restrict access to Kittal. And there was Zhina and Gaexon. His dragon senses were heightened now and they both smelt odd to him but he was being drawn to them because of it.

The air grew tenser around him and he couldn't face another fight with his brothers so retreated back to the ground.

Twenty-Five

She had lived in a daze for a few days. She couldn't believe she had finally done it, produced the child she and Canaan had craved. Together, she, Canaan and the baby had lived in their own little world and she didn't even notice that he was occasionally distracted for he would turn and smile at her before she could notice. It felt like back when they had first admitted their feelings for each other and her father had approved of their relationship. He was loving and caring and cooed over their daughter.

It finally dawned on her that her father hadn't come to admire his first grandchild and that she and Canaan had still not named their child. She turned in her chair to where Canaan was softly humming to their daughter. Already she had charmed her like he had charmed her mother. She also seemed to enjoy being in her father's arms as if she could sense the nervous tension in Tania's. She didn't want to disturb the scene but she had to for there was something amiss, there was a tension in the atmosphere she had only just noticed, "Canaan?"

"Hmm?" He turned to gaze at her and realised she had finally noticed that the house didn't feel as joyous as it should be.

"Why have you not named her yet? She is strong."
She saw a nervous twitch of a muscle in his face and he turned to put their child in the cradle. With growing fear she demanded, "why has my father not come to visit?" She stood, "where is he? What's happened?"
He pressed her down into her chair, "I haven't told you because I wanted us to remember this time for our miracle…." And he hadn't named their daughter though he had every right to for he

164

wanted to give that honour to his Nejus.

"Tell me." She ordered.

"He's alive..."

She sighed and relaxed a little.

"But he's not in great shape. Lulizen is here."

"Why? What has happened? I want to go to him." She demanded.

He hesitated. Did he refuse her? Reluctantly he said, "come then."

"We are taking out daughter with us so she can meet her grandfather." Revealing the same stubbornness that her father occasionally showed.

Together they crossed the yard. Tania was shocked to see the scaffolding on the barracks. She realised she had been cloistered away from everything, "what happened?"

"Umm, Kite crash-landed on it."

"Where is my father? Why isn't he in the house? Why did Kite crash on to the barracks?" She turned on Canaan, squeezing their daughter a little too hard and making her cry.

He sighed, "Kittal and Myrskyr tried to return him to the heavens. It failed. He is in the barracks as that was the nearest building and I didn't want you to stumble on him without knowing."

She didn't know whether to be angry with her husband or grateful that he cared enough to temporarily hide it all from her. She gave him a tight smile, "thank you."

"No one knows what happened up there yet." He remarked as he guided her round the workers calling to each other on the scaffolding.

She broke away from Canaan as they entered the barracks and headed to Harim's rooms. She slowed as she reached the door, hearing a voice inside. Cautiously she approached and looked in. Her father lay pale against pillows with his eyes closed. A hand lay on top of the blankets. His other hand was being held by Lulizen dressed in Kittal's clothes who was softly talking to Kittal and the baby gurgled at the end of the bed.

Sensing a presence Lulizen looked and a smile spread

165

across her face, "I was wondering when I would see you and this is…?"

"She doesn't have a name yet." Tania admitted, "who is this?"

"This wiggly thing is Ioan. How are you?"

"I'm all right but I promised father that we wouldn't try again." Tania glanced up as Canaan appeared.

"How is he?" Canaan enquired.

"He woke up briefly but has gone back to sleep." Lulizen answered, "as soon as he's strong enough I'm taking him back to the Valley." She didn't care what the God did, Kittal was more important to not just her but the whole of Keytel.

Canaan nodded though he didn't want to think about what might happen if he got stuck with Myrskyr.

It was another week before Kittal was awake for more than an hour and Lulizen stayed with him most of the time. She had him moved into the house now that Tania was aware of the situation and had a bed made up in his rooms so she could tend to him and Ioan. She also worked through the papers he had left scattered across the table, getting rid of anything that needed urgent attention.

She defended her family like a she-dragon and refused Myrskyr access to Kittal. He could understand why but it was frustrating as he needed to talk to him. He hoped Kittal would be able to explain why he had been unable to get into the heavens. Apart from his brothers tormenting him, none of the other Gods had made contact. None of them wanted to help him.

He watched from the end of the corridor as Kittal's family plus Diego and Harim came and went. Occasionally Zhina and Gaexon joined him. At first they tried to get him to go with them and when they couldn't they just stood with him in his silent vigil. They worried about him. Zhina thought he was retreating into himself again and she didn't want that.

It was Gaexon keeping Myrskyr company when they watched Tania and Canaan, and Diego and Harim all disappear into Kittal's room. They looked at each other as Myrskyr asked, "what do you think is happening? He hasn't got worst has he?"

"Not that I'm aware of." Gaexon answered carefully. He had an

166

idea of what was happening as he had heard murmurings amongst the Suwars about Kittal going home to the Valley, but he wasn't sure where Myrskyr fitted into it so didn't say anything.

"Perhaps we should see if we can hear anything." Myrskyr suggested and began to move towards the door.

"No, wait." Gaexon grabbed him, "look a servant is coming." They watched the servant enter with a tray of drinks and food and then leave empty handed before creeping up to the closed door. In whispers Gaexon asked, "can you hear anything?"

"Sssh, I'm trying to hear." Myrskyr hissed, ear pressed against the door.

Inside the room everyone was grouped together at one end of the room while Kittal slept at the other. Ioan and his cousin slept together in another room, watched over by a maid. They were all in reluctant agreement that they needed to get Kittal home but when and how.

Lulizen wanted Kittal home now though she was realistic. He looked even worse than when he had taken on Tania's broken back. His age was showing on him. Though there were moments when he was alert there were other times when all he wanted to do was sleep as if a part of him had been broken and not even Ioan could make him smile. She hated the fact that he had given everything but his soul but it hadn't been enough and the god wandered round as if nothing had happened.

Harim frowned as he considered all the logistical issues. Kittal was in no fit state to ride a dragon so the only option was by foot and that would take several weeks and he didn't have enough Suwars to protect a slow moving group. He remarked, "we can't get him home, not safely."

"We have to, somehow." Lulizen challenged.

"Can we not tie him to Kite's saddle so he won't fall off." Canaan suggested. He felt them all staring at him as if he was mad and he added, "it's only an idea."

"He's not well enough." Tania protested, especially as she and Canaan still needed him to name their daughter and then help her ensure she never conceived again.

There was a heavy sigh from the bed and they all froze.

They turned to the bed where Kittal shifted and cleared his throat, "are you talking about me?"

"No…. Yes." Lulizen said as his gaze fixed on her. She blushed as she admitted, "we were discussing how to get you home."

He gave her a tight smile before remarking, "you'd best let Myrskyr in."

"What?" They wondered if he had gone mad.

"He's listening outside the door."

"How do you know that?" Diego asked in astonishment.

As Canaan went to the door Kittal explained, "because you are trying to keep him away from me Lulizen. I know because I haven't see him but I do need to see him. I need to talk to him and I agree with Lulizen, I need to go home. I need to look through my books."

"No, to get well." Lulizen said sternly as she crossed the room to him.

By the door Canaan had opened it to the two young men who clearly looked like they had been caught in the act. They shifted uncomfortably under Canaan's annoyed gaze. Abruptly Canaan said, "you'd best come in."

They shuffled in, looking towards the bed where Kittal now sat propped up. Both looked shocked at Kittal's appearance. Kittal gave them a tight smile, "you look well."

"I'm sorry sir." Myrskyr said as he approached the older man, trying not to shrink under Lulizen's glare.

"How are you sir?" Gaexon carefully asked, also wary of Lulizen's glare.

"Could be better." Kittal remarked more brightly than he felt, "I need to talk with you Myrskyr."

"I know." Myrskyr looked down.

Kittal marvelled at the young man before him. As a God he had all the confidence of one but as the young man he was nervous and unsure of himself as if he couldn't cope with all the added emotions of a man.

Harim, trying to be kind, but it still came out sternly said, "I think it's time you told us what happened up there."

Myrskyr turned to look at the group and hesitated. They

168

were all looking at him and he just wanted to run and hide away
from them. He could sense all of their emotions heading in
waves towards him. He could sense the awe, the disgust, the
hatred and the love. The love confused him as it radiated from
Gaexon.

Tania crossed her arms, "come on."

He gulped, "I was so close to reaching the heavens but it was
like I reached the end of a rope just short of it and it pulled me
back. My brothers wouldn't let me re-join them." He shifted his
feet. He turned back to Kittal and asked, "why?"

"I don't know." Kittal said as he sipped at the cup of water. He
had not been visited by any Gods to give him a clue. He needed
to get back to the Valley and look through the oldest books and
scrolls in his library. He had to hope that one of his ancestors had
had to do the same as he was doing now, "I just need to get back
to my home."

"I'll carry him." Myrskyr exclaimed eagerly, suddenly feeling
that it was one way he could show his thanks.

The others frowned, unsure of the offer, considering when he
changed into a God he kept getting into fights so would Kittal
actually be safe?

"I'll stay low enough below the clouds that my brothers can't
lure me into a fight." Myrskyr promised.

Reluctantly Lulizen said, "thank you." Then sternly she went on,
"but if he dies then I will kill you, damn the consequences."

Shaking a little at the thought Myrskyr nodded.

Kittal reached out a hand to Lulizen, "don't be too rash."

She turned to look at him and murmured with fear and love, "I
just don't want to lose you yet."

"And I don't plan to die yet either." He squeezed the hand lying
on the sheets. Turning to the others and with authority said, "the
decision is made. Let's head off in two days time. Now I need to
speak with Tania and Canaan." He looked to them and they
knew now was the moment.

Everyone filed out. Lulizen made to go as well but Kittal
kept hold of her hand, "you can stay."

"Are you sure?" There were times when she didn't feel like
part of the family though they had all known each other for nine

169

years now. She knew that the relationship between Tania and Kittal and Canaan would always be stronger than the one she had with Kittal though he would disagree.

"You are my wife, don't be silly. There is nothing to hide."

Tania and Canaan came to stand at the end of the bed, holding tight to each other's hand. He looked sternly at the pair, "I don't know whether to think you foolish or to be honoured. You shouldn't have left your daughter without a name for so long." He couldn't help smiling though, "and how is my first grandchild?"

"Noisy and hungry." Tania smiled, "you can hold her later if you want."

"That would be nice. And before I go I'll give you something so you can't conceive again."
Tania blushed, "thank you."

"Bring her tomorrow and we'll celebrate." He would make the effort and get up however weary it would make him.

Tania and Canaan organised a dinner to finally celebrate the birth of their daughter. The audience chamber was filled with officials from the town and friends talking, laughing and dancing. Servants weaved through the party with trays of drinks. The Suwars, grouped around Harim, were quieter, more concerned for their Nejus, apart from the three who had created relationships with members of the local community. They didn't feel like celebrating quite so much.

Silence descended as the doors opened to reveal Kittal standing in his red robe leaning on Diego and with Lulizen on his other side. Whispers broke out amongst the women as they had never seen the Nejusana before and were surprised how young she was. They had expected a woman the same age as Kittal.

Behind them walked Tania and Canaan dressed smartly. Canaan wore a waistcoat and coat and Tania was in a bodice and skirt and wore a new pendant necklace at her throat. Tania held their daughter. They came to stand beside Kittal and Lulizen and handed their daughter over to Kittal. To the audience, with a smile, Kittal said, "I have the honour of presenting my first

170

grandchild, Bijou, the jewel of her parents' eyes."
There was a round of applause as Tania took her newly named daughter back from her father, "thank you."
   "I hope you are happy with the name." He quietly said.
   "I am." She smiled.
   "Now, go and enjoy the celebrations."
   "And you?" She asked with concern.
   "I'm going to politely decline."
She saw his eyes closing and he grimaced. His face looked paler. It had obviously taken a lot out of him just to be up. Already he had spoken with her and told her to take a tansy infusion to ensure there were no more pregnancies.
   "I don't think you should go." She remarked with fear, "look at you. You aren't fit to go anywhere."
   "I have to go Tania." He answered sternly.
She tried to hide her disappointment by giving him a kiss on the cheek and a tight smile.

Twenty-Six

Flying, tied to Myrskyr's back, hands clinging to the feathery mane and with lightning crackling high above their heads as the clouds followed them; felt like a dream. Lulizen rode with Katerina while Zhina and Gaexon rode with other Suwars. He didn't remember any of the stops made as Diego led the large group across the sea and land towards Keytel.

Kite flew alongside Myrskyr, not letting her Nejus out of her sight. Myrskyr was very aware of her. Though he knew she was by his side he still found himself drawn to the crackling clouds. He wanted to be up in the clouds with his brothers. He would become transfixed by the flashes of light within the clouds and find himself heading that way. With a shake of his head he would remember who he was carrying and retreat again.

Finally they came upon the Valley and everyone became excited even though they were all feeling tired. They found the strength to push on and reach the centre of the Valley before night fell.

Below them the village lookout spotted the group of dragons and hurried to let the villagers know. With excitement they gathered and headed to their Nejus' home to welcome him back. They knew he had been on an important mission and the fact he was returning must mean he had been successful. They were intrigued by the dragon that accompanied the group. They hadn't see one like it before.

The Suwars based in the Valley gathered on the lawn with the villagers all eager to hear how their Nejus' task had gone. They knew that something had happened to him considering Lulizen had been fetched and could only pray he was well.

Faces fell and the gathered people grew sombre as the dragons began to land. They saw that no one was on Kite's back. They wondered who was with the Suwars as they were helped down from the dragons' backs. They silently watched as their Nejusana, Ioan in a sling against her chest, was helped down. Then their eyes looked skywards at the last dragon circling, who was blending in with the dark clouds that had followed them.

As the dragons made space the dark purple dragon descended and landed on the lawn, staring round as the Suwars that had accompanied them hurried across to get Kittal from the God's back. He could sense there were lots of dragons in the Valley but couldn't see them for all the green vegetation. He was amazed at how green and alive the Valley was. He could sense that this was normally a happy place though he could feel everyone staring with uncertainty.

The eyes of the gathered watched as Kittal was helped down from the mystery dragon. They watched as with one arm around Diego and the other around Arno he was taken to the house. There had only ever been one other time when he had looked as bad but this time he looked his age. No one spoke the thoughts that they were thinking, what if he died?

On the veranda Ozanus clung to Da'ud's hand while he watched the scene before him with huge round brown eyes filled with fear. His mouth opened to say something but then closed again. Beside him his sisters clung to their nursemaid quietly crying. They could sense something wrong but didn't understand what. They didn't even smile as their mother approached with a tense smile. Ozanus stiffly asked, "am I now Nejus?" Lulizen's smile softened a little as she looked at her eldest, "not yet."

"What is wrong with papa?" Lylya asked as Shuang shoved a fist in her own mouth as she whimpered.

"He was very brave and was trying to help someone and it made him very tired." Lulizen carefully explained and hoped that her three children understood.

"Can we see him?" Lylya asked as she saw her father being brought across the lawn.

173

"Who are those others? Where did the dragon come from?" Ozanus demanded as he looked out across the lawn.

Lulizen sighed as she tried how best to explain to the children. Deciding what to say she said, "the dragon is a God. Your father had to go and find him. The other two are his companions that helped him until your father found him."

"If he is a God why isn't he in the heavens with the Dragon Lord?" Ozanus asked.

"I don't know."

"Mama, the dragon just turned into a man!" Lylya exclaimed in astonishment and pointed out to the lawn.

Lulizen turned and saw that Myrskyr had shrunk to his human form and Zhina and Gaexon were gathering around him protectively. The three were obviously sensing animosity and suspicion from the audience. She tried not to smile, glad that they realised they weren't going to be as welcome here as they had been in Jukirla.

On the lawn Myrskyr was surprised not to sense awe from the crowd. They didn't look impressed to see him even though he was a God. Guilt descended on him as he remembered he was the one who had caused their leader's poor health. He felt Zhina's hand taken his and she softly said, "remember you are a God and they don't matter."

He looked down and saw love and adoration shining from her face. The problem was he didn't need to convince her that he meant no harm, it was the crowd that needed to be convinced.

Slowly the three of them headed to the house where only Da'ud now stood outside, arms crossed and looking stern. He looked down his nose at them, "so you are the God?"

Myrskyr tried not to look afraid. He straightened his back, "I am."

"You'd best come in then. You might have to share a room, this is a rather full house."

"That's fine, thank you." Zhina hastily said before the two men could protest.

Da'ud led them into the house as he stiffly said, "welcome to the Valley where our Nejus lives, watching over and protecting the dragons that live here. I suggest you stay close to the house until

174

everyone is more comfortable about having you around."

"We've done nothing wrong." Gaexon protested.

"Sssh." Myrskyr hissed.

Da'ud turned on them, "I don't know what happened but the fact our Nejus arrives home injured and weak with three strangers could be considered a time of uncertainty especially with those storm clouds hovering above us unnaturally."

Myrskyr took a step backwards.

"He knew the risks." Gaexon pointed out.

"Hmpfh."

Lulizen couldn't persuade the children to sleep in their beds. They crowded on to their parents' bed as she placed Ioan in his cradle. The girls made a nest at the end of the bed while Ozanus slept with an arm protectively over his face holding his wooden sword and enclosed within Kittal's own arm. She kissed each one of them before claiming the space left for herself. She was glad to have her family all at home again and hopefully with his children around him Kittal would grow strong again.

She would have to wait to have Kittal to herself. For several nights she found herself sharing her bed with all three of their children apart from Ioan. By day the girls ran in and out, checking their father was still there. They seemed to be contented just to have their father at home. They didn't seem bothered that he lay in bed or was sat up working with Rafferty on all the correspondence and administration Keytel kept creating.

Ozanus was another matter. He could be drawn away for a little bit but as soon as he wasn't doing anything he would be found in the doorway of his parents' bedroom. It was as if as long as he could see his father he knew he was alive and that he wasn't going to find himself Nejus. He played with his food, glancing out of the room hoping his father might walk in smiling and suggesting they go for a ride on Kite.

He may only be six but he knew what he would be inheriting and how much work was involved in it. There were times when he hadn't seen his father for several days because of the amount of work he had. Other times he had sat on his father's

175

lap as he had received visitors and listened to the conversations though he hadn't understood a lot of what was going on.

Lulizen found her son standing guard at the bedroom door sternly telling Myrskyr he was not allow in. Pride filled her as her son had taken a similar disliking to the God though he probably wouldn't be able to articulate why. She heard him say, "I'm not letting you hurt him anymore than you have."

"Please." Myrskyr repeated.

"I think you should respect his request." She interrupted. Myrskyr turned, not seeing the triumphant smile on the boy's face.

"But I must talk with him so I can return to the heavens."

"He has not even started looking through his books yet so there is no point talking with him." She said sternly.
Myrskyr accepted defeat for the moment, "I'll go." He retreated into the house with Ozanus and Lulizen watching him.

With the god gone Lulizen said to her son, "you did well."
He grinned with pride. She saw that his colour was up under the pale tired stressed look he normally had since his father had returned home. He gripped his wooden sword tight and she wondered if he would have tried to use it though his training had only just begun. She crouched down and looked at him with concern.

The little boy suddenly came out and he flung himself into his mother's surprised arms. Tears ran down his face. He had been brave but now he revealed how scared he was. She rubbed his back as she held him close, "sssh."

"I don't want to be Nejus yet."

"You aren't." She tried to reassure him.

"But papa….?" He stepped backwards.

"He is getting better and its very brave of you to guard him but you don't have to all the time."

"I don't like that God." He said stiffly as he brushed his tears from his face, becoming the boy who believed he had to be an adult again.

"Come, why don't you come and have a nap with me and your papa." She softly suggested. She took his hand and led him into the bedroom where Kittal was putting papers to one side.

Kittal looked across as his wife and son entered and softly smiled, "to what do I owe the pleasure?"
Ozanus climbed on to the bed and snuggled into his father, hiding his tear stained face in his father's side as Lulizen said, "I was coming to claim some time with you but I think Ozanus needs it just as much."

"What have you been up to Ozanus? How are your lessons?"

"He's been standing guard outside the door." She answered as she got on the bed and ran a hand through their eldest hair. She gave Kittal a silent look full of everything that couldn't be said while their son was with them. Kittal frowned and nodded, understanding what was being unsaid.

He lifted his son's face up and said, "you don't need to worry about me."

"But....?" Ozanus started but his father put a finger to his mouth.

"Just being here with all of you is making me better."
Ozanus pulled his father's hand away, "when can we go flying together?"

"Soon." Kittal promised.
Ozanus smiled as he pulled his mother towards him. He liked having his parents' full attention. He closed his eyes, happy to fall asleep in the security of his parents' love for him and each other. For a brief moment he could forget all his worries that he couldn't fully understand and be a little boy.

Kittal looked on as Ozanus and then Lulizen fell asleep. It was frustrating not feeling able to get up. He felt strong inside but his body was refusing to let him have more than short bursts of energy. He could see how he and Myrskyr were affecting his family and wanted all of it to be over so life could return to normal.

For the moment the most important bit was he was home surrounded by his family; and Tania and Canaan were happily united playing happy family themselves. It felt good to be home. He didn't feel like sleeping so happily sat there watching over his wife and son sleeping.

Twenty-Seven

He was restless that night while his family snuffled and softly snored around him. He decided it was time to get up. He carefully inched out from under Ozanus and then from under the covers. He found his robe by the light of the turned down lamp and pulled it on. He stood and was relieved to find that his legs weren't going to collapse under him. They felt weak but they were holding him up.

He moved through the quiet house. He stepped out on the veranda hoping to admire the stars. He groaned as he saw that clouds hid the stars. He murmured, "I'll do it even if it kills me. I won't let them destroy this place."

"Sir?"

He turned to see Arno rubbing sleep from his eyes.

"Get me some tea. I'll be in my study." Kittal said softly, "and then you can go back to bed."

"Yes sir, thank you sir."

Kittal was pulling books from the shelves as Arno brought him his tea. He slipped out with a small smile on his face. He felt sure that soon everything would be right in the world again since his master was up.

Kittal began reading by the light of several lamps that he had lit but soon fell asleep, his head resting on the open pages of the book.

Mist descended on the room, swirling around it. Kittal woke shivering and pulled his robe around his bare chest against the cold. He looked round sensing a presence in the room. A voice spoke, *"it is good to see you up."*

178

"Who's there?"

There was a flash of golden scales and the mist was dragged with the long body. Kittal dropped to one knee and bowed his head, *"I am honoured to have your presence in my home."*

"You were so close."

"I know." Kittal sighed as he stood.

"How do I get him back up?"

"Only his brothers know the answer to that question."

Kittal sighed again and then asked, *"how can I talk to them?"*

"You can't unless they want to."

Kittal fought back his desire to scream and shout in frustration over it all, but he wasn't going to do it in front of his God. Why were Gods so fickle and selfish? It felt like the weather Gods were behaving like children and no one was discipling them. Whatever they had argued about the others were still holding a grudge for some unknown ridiculous reason.

"You have done well so far." There was a flick of the God's tail as he slowly curled round the room, having shrunk to fit the room, *"you will find the answers you need soon I'm sure. Now, rest."*

Kittal felt himself sinking willingly back into his chair and falling asleep again.

He woke when Lulizen shook him awake. She smiled down at him, "what are you doing up?"

"I didn't want to waste any more time. I went to look at the stars and found I couldn't see them."

"The clouds followed us all the way from Jukirla."

"How are the children?"

"Still sleeping." She smiled and then a sly expression came across her face, "do you think you are strong enough to go for a walk?"

His eyebrows went up.

She ran her hands over his shoulders and down to his chest and bent her head so her breath tickled his ear.

"Let me put some clothes on."

"I can wait if you can." She teased.

He stood, "be gentle with me."

179

"I will be. Go put some clothes on." She pushed him towards the door, "I'll wait here for you. Don't wake the children."

While he went to get dressed she took a look at the books he had open on the desk. The top one was in a language she couldn't understand but she could recognise what the picture that took up a quarter of the page was. Kittal's palm was covered in scars from the blood offerings he had done just like the picture was showing, a loincloth wearing man with a shadow of a dragon was pressing a knife to the palm of his hand and droplets of blood fell from it.

On the other page was more writing and another image of a man demonstrating another ritual offering up the head of a man to the sun that had the head of a dragon in it. An armoured corpse lay at the feet of the man. Lulizen shivered. She closed the book, glad that so few of the blood rituals still happened. She looked up as he reappeared and smiled.

He looked his usual self, dressed in his tunic and trousers with bare feet. He felt sure he would regret it later but he had had no true alone time with Lulizen for a while.

They headed out together holding hands, across the lawn and down a path through the vegetation. She led them to a small octagon pavilion she had had made as a retreat for herself but everyone had used it at one point or another. The hardwood floor was covered in cushions and blankets with a doll abandoned amongst them. A table was to one side for when the family had eaten together in her pavilion. A little stove with a copper kettle enabled her to make tea.

Roses were climbing up the wooden pillars imbuing the open room with their scent. The green painted shingle roof and low sides ensured it blended into the vegetation so no one knew it was there until they stumbled upon it.

They sat amongst the cushions, Lulizen in front of him resting against his chest. He had his arms round her as they carried on the conversation they had started as they had walked through the Valley, "I'm glad you came."

"I had to. Now that you are up you aren't going to try again are you?" She turned her head to look into his tilted face.
He shook his head, "once was enough. I will find another way to

180

get him up."

"How long do you think it will be? There have been complaints about the weather."
Kittal sighed, "I don't know. I can't control the Gods. Ozanus is looking pale."

"He's worrying about you."

"I'll take him out for a flight. That will reassure him that I'm going to be all right. Now, how about you? You are looking a little flustered?" He nibbled at her ear and his hands were busy pulling up the skirts of her dress.

"Well, the reason for that is sitting behind me." She turned her head and he kissed the corner of her smiling mouth.

She shifted so that he could put his hand between her legs. She felt his other squeeze one of her heavy breasts. She turned round and pulled off his tunic top before he ripped her bodice open and then buried his face into the top of her breasts. She giggled and pulled his face out to kiss him.

She could feel his erection through his trousers and went to undo the buttons. His hands ran down her back and then under her gathered skirts to squeeze her buttocks. He lifted her on to his erection. He didn't want to wait longer than he had to. He felt how wet she was and he had barely touched her.

She moaned as she took in his whole length. She could feel how thick it was and knew he had missed her. He leant forward and kissed her exposed throat and open mouth as he held her down on his swollen penis. Her back arched as they moved together while he held her in place straddled across his lap.

With a groan he came and sagged into the cushions as Lulizen slipped off and lay beside him breathing heavily. He reached for her hand, "don't ever grow old."
She smiled, "don't ever go limp on me."

"Oooh, harsh." He turned and laughed, "and I was giving you a compliment."
She rolled on to her side and propped her head up on her elbow, "how long do you think we can hide here?"

"Have we any food?"

"Yes?"

181

"Tea?"

"Yes." She grinned.

"I think that's all we need to stay here for at least one day and one night. I'm sure Ioan can survive on sheep milk for that long." He rolled on to his side and brushed a loose hair from her face, "you might as well take that dress off otherwise I'll completely rip it off later."

"I'll just tease you." She stuck her tongue out at him.
He rolled his eyes and then turned back on to his back. It had been good but now he felt tired again. Lulizen found a blanket and laid it over him before finding the robe she left here and then set about making some tea for them both.

Twenty-Eight

Myrskyr was up early. Every morning since getting to the Valley he had walked through the house observing everything that went on in it. He would watch Zhina and Gaexon sleeping like they had no worries. Looking into the Nejus' room he watched a family united in their love for each other. The human side of him wanted it for himself though he couldn't fully understand why.

This morning he had found Kittal missing from the bedroom and found him in his study, sleeping over his books. He began to hope then that he might get back home but there was a part of him that didn't want to. Away from the Empress' clutches he was seeing and feeling so much more. He had never thought being a human could be so complicated and fascinating with all its emotions.

He stayed hidden as he saw Lulizen enter the study. He listened to her invitation to go out and saw Kittal leave and return. Curious to see where they went he followed them discreetly.

He felt sure it was probably wrong to watch but he couldn't take his eyes off Kittal and Lulizen. He could sense the sexual undercurrents coming from them as they had walked along the path. It was similar to what he had sensed with Zhina and Gaexon. He wanted to know how to deal with it. He watched wide eyed as he saw Lulizen's dress being ripped and Kittal lift her on to his lap and then they moved as one body. He felt something stir within himself and felt a tightness in his crouch. He looked down in wonderment. He didn't understand what was

183

happening and wondered who he could ask for Lulizen and Kittal seemed to be enjoying themselves even as Kittal moaned.

He lingered and watched the slower lovemaking that happened a few hours later. He drew closer and watched Lulizen's naked plump body undulating under the touch of Kittal's fingers and tongue.

This time he found himself undoing his trousers and releasing his swollen erection. He touched it and gasped at how sensitive it was to his touch. He remembered how Lulizen had held Kittal's penis and gripped his own in the same way. He moved his hand up and down its length and felt it pulsating and moaned as he came.

Thankfully Kittal and Lulizen were too immersed in themselves to hear his moan or hear him running away through the vegetation. He shoved his penis back into his trousers as he ran, embarrassed by what he had done.

He ran back towards the house, running into Diego who exclaimed, "I thought you were told to stay close to the house." Myrskyr stumbled backwards, "how do you cope with all these emotions?"
Diego frowned, "what have you been up to?"
"Nothing." Myrskyr blushed and pushed pass the Suwar and retreated to the room he shared with Zhina and Gaexon.

Gaexon looked up from where he sat on the bed he shared with the God, "hey? What's wrong?"
Myrskyr pushed Gaexon on to the bed and kissed him, taking the man by surprise. Gaexon pushed him away, "what do you think you are doing?!"
Myrskyr retreated up the bed, "I… I thought..."
Gaexon asked, "what have you seen?"
"Lulizen and Kittal were naked and they were doing…. She was sitting on him and then…."
Gaexon started laughing, "you saw them having sex?"
"Is that what it's called?"
"Yes, and you got an erection?"
Myrskyr blushed.
"It's natural."
"I thought you felt the same way. They had an aura around
184

them that both you and Zhina have."

"What?!" Gaexon spluttered and blushed, "I..." He didn't know whether to be relieved that Myrskyr had sussed it or terrified. He took a deep breath to still his rapidly beating heart. The kiss had taken him by surprise but his body had reacted to it in a way that he knew it would and which it never did with the girls of the village. He beckoned Myrskyr forward, "come here. It's about being gentle at first."
Myrskyr crawled across the bed and knelt before Gaexon who was also now kneeling.

Gaexon leant in and kissed the God. He held the God's head between his hands as he pressed his lips hard against Myrskyr's. He tugged at a lip with his and then pushed his tongue into Myrskyr's mouth. They broke away to breath. Myrskyr's eyes were wide as Gaexon asked, "what do you think?"
Myrskyr declared, "I like it. I want more." He felt a little drunk on the blood rushing through his body.

"You sure?"

"Show me more."

"Undo your trousers."
Myrskyr didn't hesitate as they felt tight again like when he had been watching Lulizen and Kittal. He undid them and watched as Gaexon did the same. He looked at Gaexon's swollen member, "that's what mine did."

"You are aroused."

"What about Zhina?"

"She gets aroused differently. You would put it in her if she wanted you to."

"Can I ask her?"

"Ask me what?" Zhina asked from the doorway. Both young men turned, Gaexon covering his erection.

"Can I put this in you?" Myrskyr asked innocently as Gaexon's mouth dropped open in horror.
Zhina's eyes became transfixed on Myrskyr's erection and gulped. She did want to feel it inside her but hadn't expected it to be asked so bluntly. Blushing she said, "perhaps a kiss first."

"Gaexon has shown me how to do that." Myrskyr eagerly
185

replied.

"Have I missed something?"

Gaexon sighed, "he saw Lulizen and Kittal doing it."

"What?! Myrskyr you shouldn't have been spying." She exclaimed.

Myrskyr shrank away from the anger and whispered with fear, "why?"

"It's something that is a very intimate moment between a man and woman. It's not something you should be watching."

"Oh?" Myrskyr blushed and then shyly asked, "do you want to do it with me?"

Zhina gulped again, "I want to but..."

He reached out and pulled her on the bed between him and Gaexon. She turned to Gaexon to save her from the madness but she saw he had lust filled eyes set on Myrskyr. The air felt heavy with the scent of sex and lust and she gave into it.

Myrskyr took hold of Zhina's head like Gaexon had done his and put his lips to hers. She didn't resist and felt her limbs relaxing.

Gaexon wasn't sure whether to be excited or disappointed. He had wanted to be alone with Myrskyr but the God seemed to want to explore everything at once. He watched as Zhina lay down on the bed, drawing Myrskyr down with her.

Myrskyr sat up, unsure. He turned to Gaexon as if to ask what to do next. Gaexon saw his chance, "touch my erection."

"Why?"

"Because that's what men do to each other."

"All right." Myrskyr eagerly obeyed. He wanted to do everything and anything.

The three of them spent the rest of the afternoon exploring each others bodies till Zhina and Gaexon could take no more but Myrskyr seemed to be insatiable. He wanted to go on. He had loved touching Zhina's naked body and seeing how she reacted. He had felt how warm and wet she was between her thighs as he had entered her and was quickly reassured that the blood was natural. He had watched as Gaexon had knelt before him and taken his erection in his mouth. He had then done the

186

same to Gaexon and watched the man's reaction. He was a little taken aback by having Gaexon come in his mouth and spat it out.

Gaexon carefully took Myrskyr in the anus which he found uncomfortable and arousing. Wanting to get an idea of what it was like he took Zhina vaginally from behind who clung tight to the sheets as there had been no foreplay so he felt large in her. He found he enjoyed watching himself take her and let out a roar as he came.

He was loving it all. It was better than fighting his brothers. The sensations were primeval and so different from the violence he normally enjoyed. If life could stay like this between the three of them then he didn't want to go back to the Gods. As they lay in a sweaty tangled heap of sheets he said, "I don't want this to end."

"You'll be leaving us at some point." Zhina remarked, lying against his chest and brushing messy hair out of an eye.

"What if I never go back? My brothers don't want me up there anyway."

"You have to go. You are affecting our world." Gaexon pointed out sternly.

"Don't spoil the moment Gaexon." Zhina glared at him. Gaexon shrugged, from where he sat, naked, against the wall of the room, "I only speak the truth. I would like him to stay as well but he's a God, not a man."

Myrskyr scowled, "I can do what I want, I'm a God." He puffed out his chest, no one could tell him what to do.

Gaexon rolled his eyes. Myrskyr would realise eventually that he couldn't live forever in a continuous orgy. He yawned, "I think it's time we got some food."

"Can't we do some more?" Myrskyr's hand snaked round to squeeze Zhina's breast.

"No." Zhina sat up, "our bodies need to rest."

Myrskyr pouted.

187

Twenty-Nine

Now Kittal was up he did as he had promised Lulizen. Needing to be distracted from reading books which he hadn't translated since he was with his grandfather, he took Ozanus out flying. The little boy and his dragon were thrilled to be going flying with their father and mother. Dressed in a miniature version of his father's flying clothes he eagerly climbed into his saddle. Kite and Kittal rose into the air first followed by Ozanus on Ozi. Kittal glanced down to check they were all right as he said, "stay close; I don't know what mood the gods are in."

"The dragons are restless." Kite remarked, *"do you know why he fell from the heavens yet?"*

"No." He glanced down to his son again to check whether Ozanus would hear or not. He leant close against Kite, *"I still don't know and I don't think we will ever know."*

"Oh. How are we going to get him back up there? Are we going to try again?" She asked with concern.

"I don't know about you but I'm not going to be repeating that again. I promised Lulizen I wouldn't either. He said it was like a rope was holding him down."

"Then we need to find a way to cut the rope."

"I'm trying to. I'm going through all the books but haven't found anything yet." He remarked as he looked down as they now were flying over the grasslands where the animals were looking jittery.

"Papa?!" There was a wail of fear from Ozanus.
Kittal turned and realised that Ozanus and Ozi were falling behind. To Kite he said, *"lets go rescue them."*
Kite turned and slowed as she passed Ozi so as not to tumble her

daughter in the turbulence created by her body. She said, *"grab my tail."*
Ozi grabbed her mother's tail and held on tight as Kite slowed the movement of her tail.

"Are you alright?" Kittal called to his son.
Ozanus brightened, "yes. Can I ride up with you?"

"Just stay there." He turned back and said to Kite, *"let's head home."*

"Are you alright?"
Kittal sighed, *"I'm getting old Kite and so are you. I don't know how I'm coping. It took me four weeks to recover this time. This is the first time I've been out with you. I made my son ill with worry. I have a valley of dragons that are restless and a God to get back to where he belongs as well as ruling Keytel."*
He knew his son was still bright-eyed and a little feverish but he knew he was going to be alright. As for Keytel and his dragons, they would calm once he got rid of the damn God but that was proving hard. It had been a long time since he had last translated the books full of ancient and half obsolete rituals.

"Don't give up yet, please." She responded with fear.

"I'm not planning to yet." He looked back at his son who was laughing with Ozi, enjoying the ride on Kite's tail.

They all looked down out of curiosity as they saw villagers walking through the valley with someone in the centre of them. They were heading towards the house. Kittal sighed, it looked like more trouble was on its way. Kite didn't need any instructions as she turned and headed over them, towards the house.

Below, the group looked up as the shadow of the dragon passed over them. The man in the middle of the group was weary from travelling and his yellow robes were covered in several layers of dust and his shaved head was covered in thick blonde stubble. He stared up in horror at the dragon but looked away as he was cuffed round the head and the villager gruffly said, "no looking. You don't deserve to."
The man gritted his teeth. He'd been skulking around trying to find his way into the Valley and been caught. He tried to tell
189

them that he was seeking advice from the Nejus of Keytel but they were sceptical especially when he had said he was from Sunulanda. They would let Kittal decide what to do with him.

Kite and Ozi were leaving as the group arrived at the house. Arno was carrying Ozanus' saddle in. Ozanus edged closer to his father as they appeared. Kittal took his son's hand and murmured, "stand tall. Don't let them think you are nervous." He gave Ozanus' hand a reassuring squeeze as he saw him straighten his back.

The villagers came to a stop and parted as their dirty blonde haired Chief, Erza, the deceased Tomas' eldest, stepped through with the stranger in his hands. He tripped the man so he fell to his knees. Kittal frowned but said nothing about the treatment, "who have you got Erza?"

"Says he's from Sunulanda and has come to seek your help."

"Let him speak."

The mystic shook off Erza's hold on his shoulder and stood, "I was sent by Empress Esperanza. She believes that she has a God at court and needs your help in revealing him…." He stopped for he saw the young man he had been speaking of standing on the house's veranda, in better shape than he had been at the palace. His hair had grown back and he had filled out, "err…. That…." He had spent weeks travelling to the Valley, suffering sea sickness and begging for food, and somehow Myrskyr had got there first, but how?

Kittal turned to see who he was looking at. On the veranda stood Myrskyr with Gaexon and Zhina standing either side of him like bodyguards. He had noticed there had been a change in them the last few days. They had grown closer as if they had shared some secrets and now where there was one there was normally the other two as well. He frowned as he was still trying to work out what had happened. He could only hope that whatever had happened didn't change Myrskyr's mind about returning to the heavens. If needed he would drag the God back to the heavens himself so life could get back to normal.

He turned back to the stranger and raised an eyebrow. "He's meant to be…. How did he?"

"You're not the only one who was aware of him. He is now

190

under my care." Kittal said with warning, "and you still haven't told me who you are."

"I am a mystic and was sent by the Empress and I'm sure she would like her God back."

Kittal's eyes narrowed, "he is under my protection. If she understands her Gods then she should know that you can't lock them up and they won't reveal themselves unless they want to."

"I will be taking him back." He didn't really care but as he had come all this way he wasn't going to go back empty handed and suffer the Empress' anger.

"You are now in my country and obey my rules and requests. You can rest in the village for a few days and then you can be on your way. Erza make sure he obeys."

"Yes Nejus." Erza grabbed hold of the mystic and marched him off the lawn followed by his men.

Kittal felt eyes on him and looking down saw his son staring up with awe on his small face. He smiled down at him, glad that his son was impressed with him. He remarked, "see you don't need to worry about me."

"Who was that?"

"You don't need to worry about him. Come on, lets go tell your mother that we are back."

Ozanus broke away from his father and ran across the lawn to the house while Kittal picked up his saddle to carry in.

Myrskyr stood his ground as Kittal approached. Kittal gruffly ordered, "get out of my way."

"I know him."

"This is heavy Myrskyr and I'm not in the mood for you to finally find your backbone as a man."

Myrskyr's hands became fists and he shrugged off the hands that tried to calm him. He said angrily, "I'm not going back."

"You are going nowhere but to the Heavens where you belong." Kittal retorted as Arno relieved him of Kite's saddle.

"How did he know I was here?" Myrskyr demanded.

"I don't think he knew you were here." Kittal sighed.

Myrskyr then saw the old man that Kittal was behind the façade of authority and strength that he normally carried. He saw the long life that the man had had reflected in his eyes, one full

191

of stress, hardships and difficult decisions made as well as the joy. He didn't want to back down. He pushed past Kittal and as he ran across the lawn he changed into his dragon form and flew upwards with a roar. He received an answer from the clouds as lightning flashed within them.

He wanted revenge on all those that had hurt him even if they thought they were doing the right thing and then there were his brothers. Because of them he had suffered and now others who wanted to help him were suffering. He had two people who both loved him and he thought he loved back and at some point he would be abandoning them. He was torn.

The group of men, use to the black clouds now looked upward with fear at the sound of the thunderous roar and then the lightning in the clouds. The mystic remarked, "they aren't getting their due."

"What do you mean?" One of the villagers asked with worry.

"Quiet!" Erza ordered.

The mystic ignored him, "they need blood sacrifices and not just drops, a whole body."

"We don't do that here." Another said sternly.

"Maybe you should."

"Quiet." Erza snapped and cuffed the man.

"Maybe he's right." The first pointed out.

"You be quiet Decca." Erza turned on him.

"But if we did, maybe life would get better for us. Look at the clouds."

"You know perfectly well what's happening and we do **not** need to offer the Gods any more blood than necessary. They have been happy with our small offerings for years and we will not be returning to that time where we offered whole bodies now just because some stranger suggests we do. From now on you are not to go near this man. Leave now." Erza ordered.

"You are going to regret this." The mystic remarked.

"Shut up or I'll lock you up and gag you."

The mystic sneered but shut his mouth. Clearly he wouldn't be able to take Myrskyr back to Bakamon easily so he needed the Gods to help him. They didn't want Myrskyr back and the Empress did so it was a win-win for both sides. He knew that the

192

Empress had tried once before to influence them and she would try again and he would ensure she succeeded this time. He just needed to feed them enough blood.

Thirty

Shuang had claimed her father's lap as he sat at his desk trying to work on translating the book in front of him. She had curled up and fallen asleep sucking her thumb. The nursemaid came and claimed her much to his relief as he rubbed tired eyes. This was the last book to go through but he was struggling to concentrate. He was thinking back to the previous day. He could only hope that the Empress' mystic would leave quietly otherwise there would be violence that he wouldn't be able to control or stop. The atmosphere in the valley was volatile but so far had remained calm.

With a heavy sigh he turned his attention back to the book. He turned the page and realised it felt thicker then the others. He frowned and peered at the edge of it. It looked like two pages had been glued together. Normally he wouldn't have been bothered but he was getting desperate now. As he frowned over how to split the pages he heard shouts and then running steps on the floorboards. He pushed his chair back as a villager ran into the room, Arno following but too late to stop him.

"Nejus, sir, he's taken her." The villager wailed.

"Who has taken who?" Kittal looked to Arno.

"Sorry, I couldn't stop him." Arno said between breaths.

"The stranger. He took my little girl." The villager exclaimed as his breaths calmed, "he had been talking about blood sacrifices yesterday."

"What?! Arno, my sword." Kittal leapt from his chair, tiredness forgotten, "fetch some of the Suwars, I think we are going to need them."

The villager led the way with Kittal just behind him.

Three Suwars followed behind armed with swords and spears. Arriving in the village they found the women grouped together around one that was sobbing. A few of the older men and the boys who were almost men hung around, muttering to themselves. The villager ran up to the group of women, "are they still looking?"

"Yes."

"Did anyone see what happened?" Kittal demanded.

"She was playing with the other girls." An older woman from the group stepped away from it and approached Kittal and the Suwars, "and they then came running saying the stranger had taken Elsina with him."

"Where did they go?" Kittal asked.

"Where's Beneditta?" The elder woman turned to the group of women. A little girl was pushed out of the group. She tried to retreat, thumb in her mouth and wide eyed, but came up against the women's skirts.

Kittal crouched and gently said, "Beneditta come here."

"Nejus." The girl edged forward and bowed her head.

"Beneditta, I need to know where the man took your friend?" She played with the hem of her dress and stared at the ground.

"She's not going to be in trouble."

"He asked if any of us wanted to go see the dragons. Elsina said she did. I tried to tell her we shouldn't but we couldn't stop her." She began crying, "I'm sorry. Is she going to be all right?"

"We'll find her. Did they go towards the valley?"

She nodded her head.

Kittal stood and asked the woman standing behind Beneditta, "is that where the men have gone?"

"Yes."

Kittal turned, "does he know about the old temple?"

Elsina's father shrugged, "I don't know. It depends..."

"Never mind." Kittal stopped him and said to his men, "we are going to the temple."

"Yes sir." The three Suwars said in unison.

"Lets go." Kittal passed through the Suwars and led the way back into the valley.

They made their way through the valley and up the path

195

that led to the old temple. Flower petals, dried and curling up lay caught in the cracks of the stone floor left over from the Blood Moon Festival. The banners hanging from arches supported by pillars carved with dragons spiralling up them, still looked new with only a few rips in them from the wind.

At the other end stood the mystic and Elsina. The girl tugged at the hand holding her tight, screaming. The mystic turned and snapped, "quiet!"
Elsina's mouth shut and she froze in fear as the mystic pulled a knife out.

With the girl quiet he looked round. He was disappointed in the condition of the temple, clearly Keytel weren't bothered about honouring the Gods. The roof had gone and no care had been taken to maintain the temple. The altar had its stone bowl but the eternal flame had long gone out though wet ashes lay in a thick sludge in the bottom of it.

He swept off the leftover offerings on the altar with disgust. The bloodstains on the stonework had long been cleaned off by wind and rain. He looked forward to putting new blood on the stone and therefore proving the priests wrong. If they hadn't pushed him out of the school he wouldn't have had to become a roaming mystic but here and now he would rise above them all. It was a pity he didn't have the four assistants that were needed.

He picked the girl up and dropped her on the altar. She tried to wiggle off as she spotted rescuers. Seeing her eyes staring over his shoulder he turned.

Seeing men advancing he grinned, "excellent, some help is much appreciated…." He then spotted the swords in their hands, "oh?"

"Let that girl go." Kittal ordered, a tight grip on his curved sword.

"The Gods must be honoured and you are clearly not doing it." He gestured round the temple.
One of the Suwars growled.

"Let the girl go." Kittal demanded, his eyes fixed on the knife the Mystic held. He wasn't going to justify how he ruled to some stranger who didn't know the ways of Keytel.

Elsina slipped off and went to run but the mystic priest

grabbed her. She screamed and twisted in his grip. He pulled her round and held her against his front with his knife at her throat. No one moved. Everyone's eyes were on Kittal to see what he would do.

Kittal wished he had his knife but he was waiting on a new one being made by Erza. With his knife he would have thrown it and probably taken the mystic in the upper chest or throat and therefore save the girl. There were his powers but he didn't feel strong enough to use those. He'd barely done any meditating recently. All he had to use was his sword and that was useless at the moment.

The Suwars could sense him hesitating. They could see the fingers of his free hand itching for his knife which he didn't have. They wished they could hand him theirs but the mystic would see it happening. They glanced at each other, who had the best knife throwing skills?

Above them the clouds were beginning to swirl in anticipation. Lightning crackled. A wind swept through, spinning the dried flower petals and the banners flapped, briefly hiding the mystic and girl. The mystic took it as a sign. He shouted, "O Dragon Lords take this sacrifice..."
He slit the girl's throat. The scream that started as the blade dug into her soft throat ended abruptly.

The Suwars ran forward through the flapping banners and sliced the mystic down. Kittal slowly crossed the temple and stared down at the two bodies, the blood pooling together and running along the cracks. The Suwars stood round, blood dripping from their swords, waiting for their leader to say something.

Kittal looked upwards. He thought he saw bulges within the clouds that indicated the Gods were now riled up with blood. The wind briefly dropped and then rose again. Forks of lightning split the sky and one hit the cliff top further down the valley. The Suwars jumped but Kittal didn't even flinch. He hadn't seen any of this coming but now he was ready for it. The end of his task was coming and the valley was going to have to defend itself from the power of the Gods.

He turned his eyes away from the bodies, "chuck the

man's body over the cliff and let the scavengers have him. Return Elsina to the village."

"What are you going to do?" One of the Suwars asked.

"Prepare us."

"Prepare us?"

"The Gods are now hungry for more blood and they'll take their own and anyone who gets in their way." He turned and headed into the valley to find Lupe.

The conversation began with just Lupe, a red dragon, and Kite present, with Ozi shielded by one of her mother's wings, but soon others gathered. They heard that their Nejus was planning something and they had sensed a change in the atmosphere of the valley. As the group had grown larger Kittal had turned to speak with all of them, *"please don't do anything yet, just be prepared."*

"This is our home, we can't let them destroy it." A young dragon protested.

"And we won't let them though they are gods." Kittal answered firmly, *"but we must do it calmly. The Gods will win if we are gung-ho about it."* He looked at all the dragons, *"it's going to be tough and men and dragons are going to die."*

"And you?" Lupe asked.

"I must find how to get the Thunder God back to the heavens and maybe he can stop this before it happens."

They could see Kittal really was worried and knew that he was forewarning them for a reason. They looked to Lupe as Kittal left them. Lupe said, *"we do as he said. How many youngsters have we currently got?"*

"About twelve I think." A brown dragon, with green stripes on its back, answered.

"We need to get them out of the Valley." Lupe ordered.

"Are we really going to go up against the Gods?" Another asked.

"It seems so."

"We aren't going to win." The second exclaimed.

"Have faith in Kittal." Kite snarled, *"he wouldn't have come to talk with us if he didn't think we could do it. They are dragons like us. The blood making them strong will wear off."*

198

There were grumbles.

"Quiet!" Lupe snapped, *"he has asked for our help and we will give it as this is our home as much as his. We have always trusted him and we will continue to trust him. Go now and prepare yourselves and your families."*

With them gone he turned to his mate, *"we must get Ozi out of here as well."*

Kite nodded in agreement, *"I will sort it."*

"Are we doing the right thing Kite? Perhaps I should be leading all of us away from the valley and finding us a new home." He would never reveal his concerns to anyone other than his mate.

"No." Kite said firmly, *"we can't leave them now. They have looked after us for so long. Now is the time to protect them from our kind."*

Lupe willingly backed down, reassured by his mate that they would all make it and to have faith in their Nejus.

He drank the cup of water offered to him by Arno and then threw it out on the lawn where it smashed. Arno retreated a few steps. He had seen Kittal angry before but this felt different. There was a tension in the air that could make anyone a little irate. It had already got to Kittal's daughters. They were still squabbling now.

Arno looked up at the moving black clouds which seemed to have sunk lower. Lightning flashed in them and then streaked out. He watched the wind blowing the vegetation around. It was the sort of weather where any minute now it would normally rain but it hadn't happened so far... until now. Big fat raindrops began to fall, slowly at first and then it turned torrential.

Kittal turned and stared with growing frustration. He gripped the banister, trying to control his anger at the Gods. He couldn't believe he was thinking it but the Gods needed to learn to control their tempers and forget their petty squabbles. All this was happening to his Valley home because of a petty squabble.

He turned away from the scene, pretending he hadn't heard the roar of two dragons as they began to fight with each

199

other and headed to his study. Arno called out, "dinner is soon."

"Not now Arno."

Lulizen appeared and she said softly to the young servant, "I'll take him something. We are all a little stressed because of the Gods."

"When will it end?"

"I'll find out what happened. Get me some of his tea and some food."

"Yes madam." Arno wasn't that reassured but he did as he was told.

With a tray in her hands she entered her husband's study and found him set with his head in his hands. She didn't mention that a group of Suwars had started fighting with each other, the tension too much for them to control. Placing the tray down she approached, "what's wrong?"

"Everything. Our new visitor took one of the girls from the village and killed her. He's dead as well now; all because of some woman far away from here who fed them enough blood to keep them angry and restless and baying for more. And now we are all going to die because of it."

"Are you not going to try any more to get Myrskyr back where he belongs?"

"I have one last chance and then I'm out of options."

"What is that?" She asked with fear.

"These two pages are stuck together. I've never noticed before, until now."

"How are they stuck together? Let me help." She offered.

He handed the book to her so she could look.

"What if we put a bit of steam to it?"

He shrugged, "go ahead."

She brought the teapot over and held the book over it. The pages grew damp but did begin to peel apart.

She smiled in triumphant but it fell as he didn't return it. He took the book from her and placed it back on his desk. He gently pulled the stuck pages apart revealing two painted images and ink that had run. With wide eyes Lulizen asked, "was that me?"

He ran his hand over the pages, "no, I think they are older. They

200

look like tear stains."

"Do I want to know what it says?" She asked with fear.

His heart was sinking. One of his ancestors had had to do something that they hadn't wanted anyone else to go through like they had.

"Please don't read it." She pleaded. She feared what might be revealed.

"I have to." He looked at her while the hand that lay on the book shook.

She didn't want to hear it but she needed to hear it. She gulped and forced her hands to remain at her side so they wouldn't cover her ears. Her imagination went into overdrive and all of her ideas were nightmarish.

He cleared his tight throat, "if a God falls to earth then he must be returned before the world descends into chaos." He glanced at Lulizen but she didn't reveal her feelings. He went on, "the greatest sacrifice is needed. The innocence blood of a Nejus' new born is needed. If there is no child of a suitable age then himself." He struggled to say the last words and now knew why the pages had been pasted together.

Lulizen dropped to the floor with a sob of despair, "noooo!"

He slipped from his chair and joined her on the floor. His face mirrored his wife's, tears rolling down his face. She looked into his face, "please, you can't, you mustn't."

"I don't want to either."

"There must be another way." She reached up for the book and it fell from the desk. She turned it over and desperately turned the pages searching for another solution.

He took the book from her shaking hands, "we need to decide."

"No, no." She shook her head.

He put her hands on her head to stop her. She leant into him and mewed.

"It's me or Ioan…. And the book says it must be Ioan as first choice."

"Our baby…. He'll never grow up."

He wanted to stay and mourn their coming loss but he had to inform Myrskyr and then unwillingly prepare himself. He slowly pushed Lulizen away and she slumped to the floor. He

201

picked her up and carried her to their bedroom. Lying her on the bed she rolled away from him and curled up. He put a hand on her shoulder and it flinched under his touch.

Feeling her rejection in the movement he slipped from the bedroom and made for the room Myrskyr was sharing with his companions. He walked in surprising the three of them. They had all been knelt on the bed looking out with Zhina remarking, "it was raining like this the day you fell from the sky."

"Myrskyr." Kittal said sharply.

Myrskyr turned.

"Get ready to return to the heavens at dawn."

Myrskyr frowned, "what if I don't want to?"

Kittal's eyes narrowed.

"I want to stay here with Zhina and Gaexon and live together and have sex."

Zhina and Gaexon blushed under Kittal's gaze. He asked, "what has been going on here?"

Zhina opened her mouth but Kittal held up a hand, "you know, I don't really care. Myrskyr, you are going back to where you belong tomorrow morning."

"No I'm not." Myrskyr declared.

Kittal took a deep breath before grabbing the man and pulling him from the room.

Taken by surprise Myrskyr couldn't stop himself from being dragged through the house and out into the rain. He stared upwards as Kittal pointed and shouted, "you are going home whether you like it or not. If you don't my home will be destroyed. My family is going to be torn apart because of you."

"I don't want to."

Kittal turned on him and angrily said, "I'm having to do something I don't want to do. To get you up there I'm going to have to kill my son."

"Then don't and I can stay here." Myrskyr offered.

"Did you not hear me?" Kittal snarled, "you are going up and stopping your brothers from destroying my home. Do you understand me?!"

Myrskyr shrank away from Kittal and meekly said, "yes."

"Good."

Myrskyr fled.

Kittal sank to the ground, into the mud and howled out his rage.

Eventually he got up and ignored the fact he was soaked through as he moved through the house. He gave the servants orders before heading to the bedroom. He lifted Ioan out of his crib and wrapped him in several blankets to carry to his gazebo. He shielded his son from the rain until he reached the cover of the gazebo. He lit the brazier that was rarely used and stripped off his wet clothes. He sat cross legged with his son between him and the brazier.

He drew in several slow deep breaths to calm himself and to bury the anger he felt towards the Gods including the Dragon Lord. He closed his eyes so he didn't have to see his son stirring within the blankets. By morning he wanted to be ready for the biggest sacrifice of his life.

Thirty-One

She woke before dawn though it didn't feel like it was going to ever get light. Her eyes felt swollen from all the crying. She sat up and realised she was alone in the room. She called for her maid. Today she would have to be strong and stoic for her husband however much she didn't want to be.

She pulled off her crumpled clothes as her maid entered with a bowl of warm water. She asked stiffly, "where is my husband and son?"

"I don't know."

"I need my official robes."

"Yes madam." The maid bowed her head and went for the chest that held her mistress' robes.

"Get the Nejus robes ready as well."

"Arno is sorting them out."

"Has Arno seen him?"

"I don't know." The maid said as she helped Lulizen into a clean dress and then her red robe embroidered with gold dragons. Normally she would be proud to wear her robes but today they weighed heavy on her shoulders.

Arno appeared with the Nejus' robes and looked round, "is he not back yet?"

"Where is he Arno?"

Arno hesitated before answering, "in his place of meditation."

"Thank you. Is Ioan with him?"

"I think so. I was going there now."

"Is it still raining?"

"It stopped about an hour ago. The wind and lightning have stopped for the moment as well. It's as if they are waiting for

204

something."

"They are." She answered stiffly, fighting back new tears, "give me his clothes and I'll go." She held out her hands and he handed the clothes and robe over.

She walked carefully along the path to Kittal's gazebo, the trailing hem of her robe getting wet. She saw his scarred back and felt anger. As she got closer she realised it shook and his head was bowed. She placed the clothes apart from the robe on the top step and approached with the robe open. She placed the robe over his shoulders, "Kittal?"
He lifted his head and turned to look at her.

"Have you Ioan?" She softly asked.

"Yes."

"You're cold."

"I…." He couldn't find the words he wanted to say. He wanted to be cold to punish himself.
She reached round and found one of his hands. She laced her fingers through his before pulling him to his stiff feet. Gently she said, "time to get dressed."
He sucked in a deep breath, he was never going to be ready for what was coming but had had to try. Compared to this killing his brother had been easy.

She helped him dress and saw the robe weighed him down like hers did. She gathered Ioan up into her arms. He stirred and stared silently up at her as if he knew what was going to happen.

They moved through the valley as a united force with Ozanus holding his father's hand and dressed in a sleeveless red robe like his father's. Behind them came their two daughters who didn't really understand what was happening. Above them the clouds boiled and the lightning started up again and somewhere in the Valley there was a rockfall from where the lightning had hit the cliffs. Wind howled through the valley whipping anything loose up in its path.

Up at the temple ruins the villagers had gathered, mixing with some of the Suwars. Dragons stood behind them. All of them were on edge. Ranged along the cliff edges were more

205

dragons and Suwars on their dragons. They were ready for whatever happened after the sacrifice. All of them were silent out of respect for what was about to happen as they saw their Nejus and his family arrive.   Whispers had gone round quickly of what was about to happen

Standing by the altar stood Myrskyr with Zhina and Gaexon. Myrskyr stepped away from his friends. They had said their goodbyes overnight in one large sweaty heap. He stepped before Kittal, "I am ready. I should have been more grateful last night. You have done so much for me. Can I ask one more of you?"

Kittal barely nodded his head.

"Can you make sure Zhina and Gaexon are looked after?"

"Just ensure this Valley survives when you get up there." Kittal answered stiffly. He was in no mood to be promising anything considering what he was about to do.

"I'll do what I can."

Chief Erza stepped out of the audience and knelt before his Nejus. He held up the knife he had spent half the night finishing. Kittal took it and pulled his new dragon headed handled knife out of its stiff leather sheath. He nodded approvingly at the knife's sharp edge and the marbling from the meshing of metals in the furnace before returning it to its sheath. Chief Erza stepped back into the group of villagers.

Lulizen placed Ioan on the cold stone altar, opening the blanket he was wrapped in while tears ran down her cheeks again. She retreated to her other three children. She gathered them around her as Kittal's back straightened and he said, "Myrskyr, come with me."

Myrskyr followed Kittal and stood on the far side of the altar. There was a quiet gasp as Myrskyr stretched and grew and changed into his dragon form to fit the space. Everyone fell to their knees apart from the Nejus and his family.

Kittal closed his eyes and drew on his inner strength that he had spent all night trying to and failing to focus. He felt tears tricking down his face. He pulled his new knife out of its sheath as he glanced at Myrskyr. There was a hunger in his eyes which

206

were fixed on the beating heart in Ioan's chest. He looked upwards at the clouds that seemed to hang lower and lower, threatening everyone that were below them.

He took another deep breath and tried not to look at his son who was beginning to cry. He raised the knife and spoke loud enough for everyone to hear, *"take this offering to give you the strength to return to the heavens."*

All eyes were on Kittal so none of them saw Lulizen running towards the sacrifice until she spread herself across the altar and Kittal's knife went into her back. Under her Ioan howled. Kittal pulled out his knife as he cried out, "nooo!"

Myrskyr sensed blood and dived into it, not caring who it was. He leapt on to the altar and his body curled possessively around it with Lulizen and Ioan, pushing Kittal out of the way. Kittal fell backwards and stared in horror as the God devoured his wife and son. He saw Ozanus run forward crying, "mama! Mama!"
Myrskyr raised his head, revealing bloody jaws and snarled. Ozanus retreated and fell into Kittal's arms. Kittal wrapped his arms round his son though his eyes stayed trapped on the God.

Myrskyr began to glow. He unwrapped himself from the altar and pushed into the air, growing even larger as he did. He was halfway to the clouds when three dragons descended out of them. Myrskyr roared and thunder rolled through the valley. Lightning struck out in every direction. Whirlwinds headed towards the ground.

The saddled Suwars and dragons rose into the air to help protect Myrskyr and those in the ruined temple. The villagers cowered on the ground, covering their heads. The Suwars in the temple pushed through and gathered round Kittal and his children. They parted as Kittal slowly stood and approached the altar where what was left of his wife and son lay, blanket torn hanging off the side of the altar. He cautiously reached out to touch the bloody remains and fell to his knees into the blood that spread in the old channels. There was no way he could heal her even if he had the strength to. Da'ud held Ozanus back who looked as dazed as his father.

Above their heads four dragons chased and twisted and

207

snapped and slashed. The Suwars fired arrows but quickly realised they were just bouncing off the scales of the Gods. They found themselves dodging round lightning and trees being spun upwards by the wind. Rain began pelting down. Soon dragons and men began falling from the sky.

The brothers were at each other's throats, tumbling through the sky, bouncing off the cliff. They broke apart before hitting the ground, stomachs skimming over the treetops. They rose into the air with a roar before clashing again, blood pouring from wounds, rain rolling down their scales.

A powerful golden light appeared filtering through the black clouds. It grew brighter as it descended through the clouds turning them from ink black to grey to white. The clouds dissipated revealing the blue sky that no one had seen for two weeks.

A golden dragon formed and roared, *"enough!"*
Light flashed outwards freezing everyone. The four young gods wiggled in mid-air like snakes trapped by their necks, tails whipping. They snarled and still tried to get at each other. The Dragon Lord roared again, *"enough!"*
The four's eyes turned to their lord who said, *"you will let your brother return to us peacefully. He has been punished long enough and now the world beneath us needs to return to normal."*
They dropped their heads submissively.
  "Now go."
He released the four dragons from his hold and they whipped upwards and disappeared.

The Dragon Lord turned his attention to the two humans that were watching him. He came into land, shrinking to fit the floor space of the ruined temple. He placed his front claws on the altar and looked down at father and son who knelt before the altar. His expression was sombre as Ozanus stared up wide eyed in awe while clinging to his father's arm. Kittal stiffly said, *"sir."*
  "You have done well. Thank you for returning him to us."
  "Done well? Is that it?" Kittal spat bitterly, *"I've lost my wife*

and son because of him, because of you. I've given you my heart, body, blood and soul for nought. My reward is to lose my wife."
The god slowly blinked before answering, *"your son is well. Your wife protected him."*
A wail rose up from under the blanket that had slipped to the floor in the winds.
Kittal looked away. He didn't want Ioan, he wanted Lulizen.
As if he had read his thoughts the dragon said, *"I can't give you back your wife. She did a noble thing. She sacrificed herself for her child like any mother would."*
"You owe me." Kittal slammed a fist on the paved floor, bruising his hand
"I owe you nothing." The god replied sternly, *"take your son and be grateful."* He pushed off and rose skyward.

Ozanus had understood little of the conversation, but he worked out he would have his brother and not his mother. He pushed his father and angrily demanded, "I want mama."
Kittal didn't move. He let his son hit him for several minutes before grabbing his son's wrists and gently said, "that's enough now."
"He was a God and he couldn't save mama." Ozanus exclaimed.
Kittal said nothing. There was nothing he could say or do to bring Lulizen back.

Epilogue

Tania and Canaan slipped off the dragons and looked round in shock. Flying over they had seen the devastation wrought on the valley. There were rock falls from the cliffs, upturned trees and others looking like they had been tossed. Water lay in pools where it hadn't been able to soak through the waterlogged soil, already stagnating in the valley's heat. Dragon bodies still lay where they had fallen, vultures and crows picking at the bloated carcasses.

A pyre smoked on the lawn, a piece of red fabric lay caught on a charred log end. There was silence in the valley, not even a bird trilled. Rafferty ran out of the house, "am I glad to see you."

"What happened?" Canaan looked around. The Suwars had told them what they knew but that had been four days ago now.

"We had to burn her body without him. We couldn't bury it."

"Where is he?" Tania demanded.

"In her pavilion. He hasn't left for several days."

"Has he eaten?" She demanded.

"Food has been taken."

"And the children?"

"Ioan and the girls are with their nursemaid."

"And Ozanus?" She frowned with concern.

"Tania, you go to the girls and reassure them. I'll go find Kittal." Canaan interrupted. He thought it best he went as he didn't know what he would find.

She looked at him with fear. She nodded though she wanted to find her father.

Canaan headed quickly through the valley. He slowed as the pavilion came into view, a tray of food on the top step not touched. He felt nervous at what he might find. It was with some relief he saw Kittal and Ozanus. His Nejus lay in the cushions with his son in his arms.

Ozanus stirred at the footsteps. He reached for his wooden sword and pushed his father's arm off him. He called out, "who's there?"

"It's Canaan. Ozanus are you alright?"
Ozanus blinked back tears as he stiffly nodded, "mama is gone."

"I know and I'm sorry." Canaan came and sat down on the top step and Ozanus came and sat beside him.

"Papa won't talk to me."
Canaan turned to look at his father-by-law who's back was to them.

"I'm protecting him like mama would want."

"And it looks like you are doing a really good job. Can I speak to him?"

"He won't talk." Ozanus' face twisted up.

"Stay here." Canaan squeezed the boy's shoulder.

"Is he going to die as well?" Ozanus asked with fear.

"No, we won't let him."

Canaan headed into the pavilion and knelt beside Kittal, "sir?"

"No."

"Please, your children, Ozanus. They need you. You are scaring Ozanus."
Kittal rolled over and looked out of the door through puffy red eyes and saw Ozanus looked at him wide eyed. He had never thought he would be hit so hard by Lulizen's death. He felt drained of energy and life and not even his son's face could rouse him out of his stupor. He knew he had his children to see to but couldn't find any emotional strength to go to them. He muttered, "leave me alone."

"I'm not going to go until you agree to come with me. You need to take care of your children."

"You do it. I want out." Kittal rolled away from his old servant. With eyes tight shut he added, "my life has reached its

211

natural end. The Gods have no more use for me"

"It hasn't. You have four children to look after." Canaan pointed out sternly.

Kittal didn't reply.

"Fine, stay here till you see sense but I'm taking Ozanus with me." Canaan said harshly as he got to his feet, "he shouldn't be seeing his father like this."

"Fine."

Canaan stepped out and crouched beside Ozanus, "you must be starving, come on, lets take you home." He held out his hand.

Ozanus looked at his father and then the offered hand. His stomach rumbled and he took the offered hand. As they walked away he asked, "what about papa?"

"He'll come when he's ready." Canaan said as he paused to look back at the pavilion. He had never seen his lord and master so low and didn't know how to react himself. He hoped what he had said to Ozanus would happen but he had seen the knife lying amongst the cushions, Lulizen's blood still on the blade and handle. For now he would concentrate on Ozanus and ensure that whatever happened he would be as good a Nejus as his father.

About the Author:

I am an independent multi-genre author, writing since my teens. I don't have the money or the weight of a publishing house behind me so every sale and every review is truly appreciated.

Please follow me on Instagram @f_garstang_author for more about me and the books I have self published or am working on.

Other books I have written and are out include:

Bike Leather and Woolly Sheep
The Crusade's Secrets
Kukulcan's Messenger
The Guardians of the Valley

Fanny Garstang

www.ingramcontent.com/pod-product-compliance
Lightning Source LLC
Chambersburg PA
CBHW071401200726
48294CB00010B/1780